WINGS OF THE VALKYRIE

WINGS OF THE VALKYRIE

THE LONE VALKYRIE™ BOOK 3

CHARLEY CASE   MARTHA CARR   MICHAEL ANDERLE

LMBPN Publishing
PMB 196, 2540 South Maryland Pkwy
Las Vegas, NV 89109

First US edition, May 2020
eBook ISBN: 978-1-64202-943-7
Print ISBN: 978-1-64202-944-4

THE WINGS OF THE VALKYRIE TEAM

Thanks to the JIT Readers

Kerry Mortimer
Deb Mader
Dorothy Lloyd
Larry Omans

If we've missed anyone, please let us know!

Editor
The Skyhunter Editing Team

DEDICATIONS

From Charley

This book is dedicated to my wife and best friend, Kelly. Without her belief in my abilities, and patience to see the process through, this book wouldn't exist.

From Martha

To all those who love to read, and like a good puzzle inside
a good story
To Michael Anderle for his generosity
to all his fellow authors
To Louie and Jackie
And in memory of my big sister,
Dr. Diana Deane Carr
who first taught me about magic, Star Trek,
DC Comics and flaming cherries jubilee

From Michael

To Family, Friends and
Those Who Love
To Read.
May We All Enjoy Grace
To Live The Life We Are
Called.

CHAPTER ONE

Mila sat cross-legged on the couch, the baseball-sized device Penny had created with Rebecca and Lance cupped in her hands. She tucked her bare feet under herself, mashing them into the down-filled seat to keep them warm on the chilly spring morning.

The cold normally wouldn't be a problem, but Penny had the double French doors to the balcony open as she worked to reinforce the wards on the building, and the breeze was slowly sucking the heat from the room.

Now that Missy was firmly on Azoth's side nowhere was particularly safe, but Penny would ensure that it would take some real effort to attack the condo. The only thing they had going for the building was the fact that Missy hadn't known about Mila while she spent five years hatching the plan to resurrect the Drude and use him to take her home with his abilities. She might not have the specifics like with Victoria's secret place in San Francisco, but the elder Valkyrie knew that Mila was somewhere in

Denver, so Penny decided it wasn't worth the risk and had been beefing up security on the building for the last week.

Stretching her neck until there was a satisfying pop from her spine, Mila settled into the cushions and wiped a little nervous sweat from her hand on the knee of her leggings. She felt a chill as a fresh gust of wind made its way to her. While reaching over and grabbing a red hoodie she had draped over the arm of the couch, Mila saw Victoria sigh heavily as she turned the page of the novel she was reading.

After pulling on the hoodie, she put the device in the large pocket before zipping up the front and turning slightly to face her elder.

"Are you doing okay? You've been a little…" Mila looked the normally well-kept woman over, noting the mustard stain on the thigh of her gray sweatpants, and the very wrinkled state of the Ramones t-shirt she had been wearing for the last two days, "not yourself, lately."

Victoria dogeared the page she was on and ran her hand through her hair, but it became tangled in the long blonde locks before she had it halfway through, forcing her to back out and come at the tangle from another direction. She quickly raked out the small bird's nest, her cheeks turning slightly red.

"I'm fine, all things considered." She tossed the book to the cushion beside her and tucked her feet under herself. "I mean, it turns out that the one Valkyrie who outranks me in seniority is also the one who awoke our greatest enemy, and led the monster to multiple of our sisters so it could feed on their souls. Other than that, I'm good."

Mila pulled the device out of her pocket and ran a

thumbnail along one of the many seams. "Yeah, I get all that. I feel it too, although not to the same degree. I was thinking more along the lines of the fact that you haven't been working. As long as I've known you, you were all about your company. I don't think I've seen you make a phone call since you told the Valkyries to scatter. Aren't you worried that your business is going to, I don't know, fail or something?"

Victoria laughed bitterly. "Oh, that's all over. As far as my company is concerned, I'm dead. Missy knows too much about all that. Even my secret apartment wasn't exactly a secret to her. No, my business days are over for now. It was about time I moved on anyway." She dramatically tossed her hair over her shoulder and gave a look that was so sultry it could only come from hundreds of years of practice. "I was getting a little too old to pull off this body for much longer. If anyone took the time to do the math, they would have seen that I've been running the company for forty-three years. I may not look as young as Missy with her blue pigtails and micro skirts, but I sure as hell don't look like I'm in my sixties."

Mila snorted a laugh. At most, Victoria looked about thirty-five, the same as Mila and the rest of the Valkyries she'd met. "How did you get away with it for so long? Shouldn't people have been asking questions, like, twenty years ago?"

"You'd be surprised what people don't notice when they're making obscene amounts of money. I kept their bank accounts full, and they pretended my plastic surgeon was a miracle worker." She gave a half-smile as she stared off into the past. "This one was a good life. No spouse this time around, which is a blessing and a curse. Plenty of lovers, though, which is fun for a while but to be honest, I was getting bored by the end. There's only so much money you can make and so many strangers you can fuck before you don't care anymore."

"Have you been married before?" Mila had never considered that Victoria might have a spouse. It seemed like such a foreign concept for the woman in power suits to have someone waiting for her at home.

"Dozens of times." A sad smile touched her lips. "For us, it always ends badly, though. Well, usually. We outlive them all.

"I was married in this body, way back when I was first reborn. Grady. Grady Mays—he was an oil tycoon who lost it all in the Great Depression. Poor guy died penniless." She suddenly laughed. "He was way more fun after he lost everything. We would jump boxcars and travel across the country when his latest scheme inevitably fell through. It took a while, but I eventually convinced him we didn't need the money, and he miraculously just…let it all go. We eventually bought some land in California, back when it was still nearly empty, and built a house out of trees we cut from the property. Lived out the rest of his days in peace. He took up carpentry. I always thought that was such a weird choice. He was crap with his hands when it came to using anything more than a pen, but he loved it."

"Was he a magical?" Mila asked, completely taken by the charm of the story.

"Nope. Peabrain."

Mila cocked her head to the side. "How old was he when he died?"

"You're wondering why he never figured out I wasn't aging?"

Mila nodded.

"He was eighty-three when he died." Victoria smiled. "He never noticed me not aging because he was already twenty-five years older than me when we married. When you spend enough time with someone, you see them how you see them, regardless of how they look. It's why attractiveness is so unimportant in the long run. I think he knew something was going on, but he wasn't going to complain." She smiled. "Besides, we had fun."

The talk made Mila think about Finn and the fact that this would happen to her at some point, but it was so far in the future, she didn't know how to frame the idea. Her thoughts must have shown on her face because Victoria awkwardly cleared her throat.

"Sorry, I forget that you're still new to all this. You luckily picked a long-lived race as a mate. Dwarves can live for hundreds of years. You two will have plenty of time to be together."

Mila smiled while tossing the device from one hand to the other. "I know. It'll work out somehow."

They sat in silence for a minute, both thinking about the past and the future.

Mila raised an eyebrow as a thought hit her. "If you're done with the company, does that mean you're broke again?"

Victoria smiled mischievously. "That's one of the great things about being rich at this time in history. There are so many ways to hide money that enormous amounts can go missing and no one will notice. Like I said, I was preparing to leave for a while. I have stacks of money hidden away in offshore companies and banks all over the world. Hell, for a while in the eighties and nineties, I was making so much money that I had to make the company look way less profitable than it was so I wouldn't get noticed. It's not good practice to be a magical and run a company that pulls in ten times what the next most profitable company does. The community looks down on that, thinks you're using your powers to unfair advantage. There's a reason I've never shown up on the billionaire lists. I hide it all."

"Bill...how fucking rich are you?" Mila's eyes bugged out a little.

"Very." She pointed at the device. "Are you going to charge that, or fondle it all morning?"

Mila looked down at the dark brass-colored ball in her hands, half-forgetting she had it. A spike of unease filled her like it always did when she dumped her raw magic into it. It was unnatural how stable the thing looked considering how much power it contained.

"Yeah, sorry. I know I've been putting it off. Something about it gives me the creeps." She held the device up at eye level as if trying to peer inside its thick shell.

"I know what you mean. Between you and me putting everything we have into it every hour for the last week and the couple of dozen charges the other sisters gave it while we were cleaning up on the rooftop deck, I figure it has to have about three hundred times the power either one of us can hold on our own."

Mila nodded. "Not only that, but it doesn't let you know how much more it can hold. I keep worrying that I'll channel power into it and it'll suddenly be full. Next thing I know, I'll be spraying raw magic all over the room."

Victoria went a little white. "I hadn't considered that."

"Shir?" Penny flew in through the open doors.

"How can we tell when this thing is full?" Mila let Penny know what they were discussing.

The little blue dragon flared her wings and landed on the couch beside Mila. She pursed her lips and put her hands on her suspiciously thick hips before shrugging. "Chi chi."

"Well, that's helpful." Mila rolled her eyes as Penny flopped down onto her back, yawning.

"What did she say?"

"She said, 'when it doesn't take any more magic,' like an asshole." Mila stuck her tongue out at Penny as the little dragon put her hands behind her neck, making her belly stick out even more than it had been. Mila pointed at the distended abdomen. "What's going on here? Did you eat a whole chicken or something?"

Penny swiped a hand at her finger, batting the digit away and giving Mila a dirty look. "Shir shee chi?"

"No, you don't comment on my flabby butt, but only because it's so tight you could bounce quarters off it, and you know it." Mila chuckled. "You would be the first person to comment if I let myself go, you little hypocrite."

Penny smugly shrugged and shot a smoke ring from her nostril.

"Are the wards up to your standards?"

Penny nodded, explaining that she had upgraded the wards to make the building invisible to anyone that meant its inhabitants harm, along with a few offensive measures on the off chance that someone attacked the building.

"While I appreciate the hard work," Mila set her jaw as her eyes hardened, "I don't think we want this building to be the last stand if Azoth finds us here." She looked up at the rather plain-looking hand scythe sitting on the shelf above the TV. "We need to have somewhere to take that thing if they get too close."

"Shir shee? Chi shee shir."

Mila's brows rose slightly. "That's not a bad idea."

"What's not a bad idea?" Victoria looked between Mila and Penny.

"We can take it to Penny's friend Rebecca's house. Finn and I owe her a visit anyway, and she knows the stakes. You think she would be amenable?"

Penny nodded enthusiastically. "Shir!"

Mila laughed. "Road trip, indeed."

CHAPTER TWO

By ten o'clock, Penny and Mila had spoken with Rebecca on the phone. She was more than willing to keep the Reaper if the condo was compromised, but Penny insisted that she come and put up additional protective wards at the house. Rebecca said they should all come and have dinner so that everyone knew how to get there, and it was about time they all met in better circumstances than a rooftop battle.

An hour later, Rebecca teleported into the condo after Penny made her a recognized guest to the new wards. Mila and Penny sat with the tall, attractive witch with short blue hair at the kitchen island while Finn ran to the store to get food and beer for the day's activities.

Danica stumbled out of her room, her arms reaching far over her head in a giant yawning stretch. She wore a pair of gray jersey cotton shorts and a cropped t-shirt that was riding so high that it exposed the bottoms of her breasts. The long-legged elf spotted their guest and imme- diately dropped her arms, turning bright red.

"Oh my God, I didn't know we had a guest," Danica sputtered while trying to pull the cropped tee down to her waist, but it wasn't going to happen.

Rebecca laughed and stood to shake Danica's hand. "Don't worry about it. I have a set, too—I know what they look like. I'm Rebecca, Penny's friend. You must be Danica. Penny talks about you a lot."

Danica took her hand and shook, but looked past Rebecca to catch Penny blushing from the fruit bowl she was using as a recliner. "I hope it's all good?"

"I don't think she's ever said a bad thing about you."

"Well, it's good to know she reserves all her snark for face-to-face interactions." Danica stuck her tongue out and winked at the chagrined dragon. "Is there any more of that coffee left? I worked a twenty-four-hour shift last night and didn't get to bed until six a.m."

"There's a couple of cups left. I just brewed it." Mila sipped her brew as Danica went around the island and pulled her favorite mug from the cupboard. "Are you busy today?"

"Not at all." Danica filled the cat-covered mug and inhaled a deep sniff of the vapors. "Last night was the end of this month's Emergency rotation. I have the next four days off."

"Are you going to be hanging out with Phil?"

Danica shook her head. "He's at a conference in D.C. this week. It always happens this way. I have time, and he's gone. He has time, and I'm working. I'm half-tempted to quit my job so I have time to hang out with my boyfriend." Danica chuckled and sipped loudly. "Oh, yeah...that's what mama needed," she moaned into her mug.

"Well, you should come with us to my house," Rebecca suggested, sitting back down on her stool. "We have the pool, and it's a beautiful day for drinking on the deck."

"Plus, we're going to grill out for dinner." Mila waggled her eyebrows. "It's your favorite…"

"Scallops?"

Mila's brows dropped. "Oh, I thought your favorite was shrimp."

Danica laughed. "I love shrimp, especially with steak."

Mila brightened. "Well then, you're in luck. Finn is at the store right now getting everything. Knowing him, there will be filets for everyone along with more shrimp than you can shake a stick at."

Danica smiled. "I don't know. I can shake a stick at a lot of shrimp." She looked Mila up and down, then checked out what Rebecca had on and turned back to Mila. "Are you going to wear that? It doesn't scream day in the sun like Rebecca's sundress."

Mila looked down at her leggings and red hoodie then over at Rebecca, who was pulling off a yellow sundress that perfectly complemented her short, dark blue hair.

Mila gave Danica a helpless look and slowly shrugged. "Uh…no?"

Danica laughed and rolled her eyes. "I'll go pick something out for you. Did you pack bathing suits?"

"Not yet." Mila gave Rebecca an apologetic look. Rebecca smiled while stifling a laugh.

"Where's Victoria?" Danica headed around the corner into the dojo on her way to Mila's and Finn's room.

"She's showering," Mila called and hiked a thumb at her

old bedroom they had converted to the guest room, although Danica couldn't see the gesture.

"About time. That girl has been moping on the couch for three days. I'll get her something to wear from my closet."

The sound of the bedroom door opening let them know that Danica was out of earshot.

"Does she always pick out your clothes?" Rebecca quickly hid her amused smirk with her coffee mug.

"Only when she wants me to look like an adult. I'm pretty useless when it comes to fashion." Mila was a little self-conscious in the face of yet another woman who understood how to pick out and wear clothes.

"It can't be that bad." Rebecca chuckled. "Your leggings are nice. They sculpt you perfectly, and if I'm not mistaken, they're designer."

Mila looked down at the black leggings and had to admit that they were rather fetching, with their intricate stitching and gauzy semi-see-through panels at the side of the thigh and calf. "Yeah, they are pretty badass..." she slowly looked up with an exaggerated sad smile, "but Danica bought them for me. I didn't know they were designer until now."

Rebecca threw her head back and laughed, making Mila laugh along with her.

"You were right, Penny," Mila acknowledged with a dip of her head, "I like her a lot."

Penny gave her a smug smile.

"Holy shit," Finn said in slack-jawed amazement as he slowly spun in a circle taking in Rebecca's house from where they had appeared on the deck, "you live in a treehouse! Fu…" he suddenly stopped, seeing Grimm sitting at the kitchen table, well within earshot of where they stood on the deck, "uun… Fun me."

Everyone stared at the tall dwarf as he slowly turned a little red before hiking up both hands holding the combined twenty or so plastic grocery bags filled with meat, beer, and various sundries for side dishes. "Where should I put these?"

"Bring them inside," a short man with curly blonde hair said as he stepped around the kitchen island. "I'm Lance. You must be Finn."

Mila watched as a big smile spread across Finn's face. "Hey, Lance. Nice to meet you. You must be Grimm," Finn added as he walked past the table and gave the curly-haired boy a big smile.

"Yup!" Grimm announced and waved a jelly-stained hand after carefully setting his PB&J on a plastic plate with a cartoon character smiling up at him.

Mila turned back to the others as Lance and Finn made their introductions. She took a moment to admire the amazing house. It was made of glass and steel with a single large wooden deck running around the perimeter and suspended between two of the largest cypress trees Mila had ever seen. Suspended wasn't quite the right word since the trees were growing through two sections of the house and the structure was built around them. Every outward-facing wall was floor-to-ceiling glass. Some rooms had gauzy curtains to block the view inside, but most of the house showed the seemingly endless sweep below it. Teak and stainless-steel outdoor furniture dotted the deck, which surrounded a large swimming pool with an attached hot tub.

"This house is amazing." Mila's eyes caught more fine details the longer she looked. "How on Earth did you get a builder out to the middle of a swamp?"

"You're still thinking like a Peabrain." Rebecca laughed. "We didn't have a builder. We created this house. We wanted something that could grow along with the trees and our family. The house itself is almost alive in its ability to shift and change as needed. This morning, the pool grew a hot tub." She pointed to the round bubbling tub situated in the deck and creating a mini waterfall of steaming water into the main pool. "I guess the house thinks we need a soak."

"That's incredible," Danica exclaimed before shouldering Mila lightly. "Maybe we should do something like this with the condo."

Mila chuckled. "I don't think this is a retrofit kind of deal. Pretty sure we would have to start from scratch."

They went inside and introduced themselves to Lance and Grimm. Mila, Danica, and Victoria all sat at the large dining table along with Rebecca, and Grimm sat at the head of the table, still finishing his sandwich.

Mila leaned in to inspect the gooey sandwich and smiled at the little boy. "It's nice to meet you, Grimm. How old are you?"

He held up a sticky hand, his fingers extended and thumb tucked. "Four! How old are you?"

Mila smiled. "I'm thirty."

His eyes went wide. "That's so old!"

Everyone laughed, and Rebecca turned a little red with embarrassment. "Sorry, he's still learning about social graces."

"It's fine." Mila pulled the large shoulder bag over her head and placed it on the table. "Hey Grimm, if you want to know about old, ask Danica. She's older than my grandma."

Danica playfully slapped Mila's shoulder. "Jerk!"

Penny landed on the table and sat in the empty fruit bowl Rebecca had obviously left out for her since there was a second bowl full of oranges and bananas. Her movements seemed a little sluggish, which concerned Mila, but before she could ask what the matter was, Lance asked in a loud voice if they all wanted a drink. Penny perked up and squeaked out her order for a Lance special.

"Sounds good to me," Mila added. She had already heard tales of Lance's drink-slinging skills from Penny's last visit.

Danica and Victoria agreed, along with Rebecca, making it a full round.

"Easy enough." Lance filled a stainless-steel tumbler with ice. "Batch drinks let us get to the drinking faster."

Mila adjusted the short sky-blue sundress Danica had picked out for her. She wasn't used to sitting in short skirts, and the sizeable amount of skin contact with the chair made her feel like she was showing way more than she was. She also felt a little naked without her corset harness on, but she felt better knowing that it was in her shoulder bag along with Finn's harness. They had both learned the hard way that you never leave home without your weapons.

Along with the harnesses were the bathing suits Danica had stuffed into the bottom of the bag. But the thing that took up the most room was the black leather-covered hard case that looked a little like a miniature guitar case if you squinted. Victoria and Finn had created it to store the Reaper and the spherical device. The scythe's thin handle looked like the neck, and the curved blade resembled the body of a foot-and-a-half-long guitar. There was a half-sphere impression in the dead space of the blade's curve where the device nestled perfectly and was held in place when the case was closed.

Seeing the black case peeking out of the bag reminded Mila about a few questions she'd meant to ask. Penny had told them that Rebecca came from a long line of historians and had more info on the Drude than even Victoria knew. From what Mila could gather, Rebecca's ancestors had taken passage on Earth to document the new races they expected to encounter at the mysterious destination of the planet-sized ship. Evidently, her ancestors already had an extensive library of notes on everything out there, but the battle between the Drude and the Valkyries that had taken place in *Earth*'s early days was something that few had witnessed. She had an entire book written on the subject from her many-times-great-grandfather named Gregory.

Mila pulled the case out of the bag and flipped the two latches before cracking it open and pulling out the device that Rebecca, Lance, and Penny had created. She still felt trepidation at holding that much concentrated power, but the device showed no reaction whatsoever. It might as well be an inert ball of brass.

"I have some questions about this." Mila set the device on top of the closed case.

The mood in the room changed a little. The only one who didn't notice was Grimm, who was licking the last of the jelly from his plate.

"Hey, honey, why don't you take your plate to the sink then go watch some cartoons," Rebecca sweetly directed Grimm, helping him out of his seat and playfully swatting his bottom as he ran to the kitchen.

"I think I'll see how the drinks are doing." Danica patted Mila on the arm and smiled at her. "I have a feeling this will take a minute. Hey, Penny. You want some of those snacks Finn brought?"

Penny considered, then nodded and launched herself from the bowl and onto Danica's shoulder as she headed for the kitchen. She had to dodge out of the way of a sprinting Grimm as he blew past her and leaped down the two steps into the large white-carpeted living room.

Rebecca put her elbows on the table and rested her chin on her folded hands. "I can tell you what I know, but the problem is that thing was only a theory until we built it."

Mila bit her lip, thinking of all the things they needed to know and feeling a little overwhelmed, but Victoria jumped in and asked the obvious first question.

"How do we know when it's full?"

Rebecca's eyes widened a little as she considered the question. "I...I have no idea. Gregory wrote that it should hold roughly ten to twenty times the magic a Valkyrie could contain at one time. I would assume you've been charging it. Is it becoming hard to fill?"

Victoria and Mila looked at each other with slight alarm. "No, we don't have any issue putting power in, but I think that estimate is off by a little." Mila rolled the ball around on the case with a finger.

"Why? How much have you put into it?"

Mila pursed her lips in thought. "Roughly three hundred full charges. Victoria and I have been dumping everything we have into it about fifteen to twenty times a day."

"Plus, the other sisters added twenty-ish charges in San Francisco," Victoria added.

Rebecca blinked in shock while looking at the unassuming brass-colored ball. "That's a lot of magic."

"No shit," Victoria agreed.

CHAPTER THREE

"I'm not as concerned by how much power is in there as I am by how it's supposed to work." Victoria crossed her arms and leaned back in her chair. "I'm pretty old, and I don't know how a Drude can steal the power from a Valkyrie. Granted, I was fairly young when I was assigned to watch over the Reaper and had only been in a couple of battles before then. My point is that I was in a war with these things, and I still don't know how they can do half the things they can. How do you know this gadget will do what it's supposed to? I didn't know Drudes came back to life until Azoth showed up again. There's a mechanic that I don't see about the Drude, and we better make damn sure it will work before we try it."

Rebecca nodded as Victoria voiced her concerns. "I have to admit that unfortunately, there's no way to test the device before facing Azoth. Unless you think he would be kind enough to show up for a test run?"

Victoria rolled her eyes. "That's not what I meant."

"I'm on Victoria's side with this one." Mila leaned her

elbows on the table. "I understand that we can't test the device, but it would be helpful to understand why your ancestor thought it would work in the first place. I don't know about you guys, but information makes me feel better, especially when my life is on the line."

Rebecca nodded in understanding and walked over to a bookshelf that separated the dining area from the living room, where Grimm was bouncing along to a musical on the large flatscreen TV. She grabbed a large leather-bound book with several dozen bookmarks sticking out of the pages.

As she sat back down at the table, Lance walked over with a tray of drinks. "Okay, three Lance specials."

"Thank you, Lance. This looks delightful." Mila beamed as she took the frosty copper mug he handed across the table.

"Thank you, babe." Rebecca reached over and casually patted his butt. It was obviously something they often did because neither one of them seemed to notice it happening until Finn laughed.

"Mila and I do the same thing all the time." He chuckled and pointed at Rebecca's hand on Lance's behind. "I told you we were more alike than you thought."

Lance laughed as Rebecca turned a little red when she realized what she was doing. "I suppose you're right, Finn." Lance looked at the three women in the midst of their intense conversation and took the hint with admirable grace. He looked up through the bookcase at Grimm dancing away.

"Hey, buddy. Why don't you put your suit on so we can swim? Mom and her friends could use a little quiet time."

He leaned down and kissed Rebecca on the top of her head. "We'll get out of your hair. You guys come out when you're done. It's too beautiful a day not to spend it outside."

"Thanks, babe." Rebecca kissed him as Grimm sprinted past them, heading farther into the house, presumably to put on his trunks.

Danica came over to where Mila was sitting and grabbed the shoulder bag from the table. "We'll head out, too. Maybe I can get a little sun for once."

Mila snorted. "Don't you use magic to keep your complexion that pale? What is sitting in the sun going to do if you're going to magic it away?"

Danica shrugged. "Maybe I'll give a tan a try. Phil recently got a pretty dark base tan for a guy who spends all his time in a basement, probably because we spend so much time doing outdoorsy stuff. He looks good with a tan. Maybe it's time I catch up."

"Are you going to stop dying your hair, too?" Mila's question caused Danica to blush slightly.

"You dye your hair?" Rebecca and Victoria asked at the same time.

"I assumed you were a high elf with the pale skin and blonde hair." Rebecca looked Danica over with a critical eye. "Are you a wood elf?"

Danica nodded, an embarrassed smile on her face. "Yeah. My parents were pretty upset when I started dying my hair."

"Were you ashamed of being a wood elf? I don't understand. Wood elves are some of the best fighters in the universe. They have everyone's respect."

Mila and Danica laughed together at the thought of

Danica being ashamed of who she was. "Danica wouldn't dream of pretending to be anything other than who she is. Usually to a fault."

"Hey!"

"If you're not hiding your heritage, then what happened?" Victoria raised an eyebrow.

"The nineties happened." Danica laughed. "I don't know if you remember, but frosted tips and pale skin was all the rage. I guess I never stopped, and now this is what I look like to most of the people I know."

Victoria nodded in understanding. "Oh, I remember the nineties. It wasn't nearly as cool as people seem to think."

"I'm pretty sure no one thinks the nineties were cool." Mila furrowed her brow.

Grimm sprinted down the hall wearing a pair of swim trunks with SpongeBob characters all over them. He let out a long, high-pitched battle cry as he flashed past the table and out onto the deck before jumping belly-first into the pool.

"I should get out there," Lance said before looking down at himself and frowning at the polo and cargo shorts he still wore.

Rebecca patted his bottom and smiled. "Go change. I can watch him for a minute."

"Thanks, babe. I was trying to give you guys some space, and now you're doing my job."

"It's fine." She patted the book lying on the table in front of her. "I need to find a particular entry anyway. It'll be a couple of minutes before we can continue."

"Do you need to go out there?" Danica watched Grimm splashing around like he'd been born to swim.

"No. If he's in trouble, I can get him from here." Rebecca pulled her wand out of nowhere and laid it on the table before opening the ancient book and scanning the pages.

"Come on, Finn." Danica grabbed his hand and pulled him deeper into the house. "Let's change and leave these nice ladies alone."

"Oh, the house put a pair of guest rooms down the hall to the right. Feel free to use them to change," Rebecca called after them, not taking her eyes from the book.

Mila watched as her best friend and lover turned the corner. Finn smiled at her and waved before he disappeared.

Rebecca seemed to be deep in her reading, hopefully looking for answers to their questions. Victoria was watching Grimm like a hawk, although Mila was sure Rebecca had some sort of spell on the little guy to let her know if there was a problem. She seemed far too put-together to let her only child be in any real danger.

Mila lifted the device, feeling the weight of it in her small hand. She hadn't filled it before leaving the condo and felt a little guilty. If this thing was the only way to take Azoth out, then she should do everything she could to ensure it was charged enough.

Seeing that the other two were busy, she decided she might as well do it while waiting for Rebecca to find what she was looking for.

Mila closed her eyes and cradled the device in both hands, resting them in her lap. She cleared her mind the way she did before meditation. It wasn't necessary, but she felt like the process went a lot smoother when she could block out the outside world while she channeled her power into the endless well within the device.

Grimm's splashing became like white noise, drowning out the sound of Rebecca turning pages and Victoria's occasional slurp of her mixed drink. When Mila felt her center calm to a mellow hum instead of its normally erratic behavior, she turned her focus to the device in her hands. She felt the nearly flush joints where the individual pieces interconnected. Pushing past the brassy exterior, Mila found the spot she liked to think of as the pipe.

The spot was tiny, but it could accept huge amounts of power and funnel it into some dark unseen core at the device's center. With a flick of her will, she channeled her raw celestial magic into the pipe, marveling at how eagerly it swallowed the power.

Mila could never tell how much time it took to funnel about ninety percent of her power into the device, but she knew it was closer to five minutes than fifteen from checking the time before and after on several previous charging sessions.

When Mila felt her magic dipping to that ten percent level, she cut off the flow and slowly opened her eyes as if she were waking from a quick nap. Mila blinked a few times and felt the emptiness of her missing magic, but at this point, she had drained and refilled her magical reserves so often that she also felt the void already starting to draw in more ambient celestial magic. She smiled at the newly familiar feeling and looked up to see Rebecca watching her.

"That was interesting." The witch's left brow slowly rose.

"What was?"

"Most magicals have access to as much magic as they need, being more of a conduit than a vessel, but you can only hold so much magic at a time. When you channeled your power into the device, I saw your aura fade along with it. It was like you were becoming a nonmagical."

"That's not possible." Victoria turned back to the conversation. "We're Valkyries. Our auras never fade. They shine from the day we're reborn, although we don't have access to our powers and memories until our late teens. It's what we are."

Rebecca smiled. "I take it you can't see auras?"

Victoria shook her head. "It's a rare ability for a Valkyrie."

"This is fascinating, but why would it matter? We know I'm a new Valkyrie, so my abilities are adapting to the situation. Maybe my aura fading as I use magic is part of some unseen ability."

Victoria shook her head. "No, you don't understand. It's not possible because you *are* the aura. We're a hundred percent energy riding in a body. The body can die and we live on, but if the energy dies, then the body goes with it. It would be like a Peabrain fading from existence the more tired they became."

"But that's exactly what the Drude do," Rebecca cut in, drawing odd looks from both women. She flipped back a page and found what she was looking for. "My ancestor Gregory, the one who was with you at the first battle with the Drude early in *Earth*'s journey?"

"Wait." Victoria held up her hand and shook her head in

disbelief. "You're telling me that you're related to Old Greg?"

"Old Greg?" Mila muttered.

"Yeah, old guy who asked way too many questions?"

Rebecca nodded. "Sounds about right. He was my great-great-something grandfather. He basically wrote the book on magicals, although he never had the chance to publish it." She patted the leather-covered volume in front of her.

"Wow." Victoria leaned back in her chair and looked up at the ceiling, her mind thousands of years in the past. "I didn't talk to him all that much. He wanted to know specifics about the Drude. I was still pretty new back then, so Missy took the lead. They talked for days."

"I can imagine, considering how much he wrote about what the Valkyries had to say. Most of it comes from a woman named…" She scanned the page.

"Brindal." Victoria filled in the name. "She was a tall, muscular blonde back then." She snorted a laugh. "The dwarves were all over her. She had to threaten them with physical harm before they got the clue that she wasn't fucking around about being married."

"Matches the description he gave here." Rebecca nodded with a contemplative look as she started reading to herself again.

"Can we get back to the subject here?" Mila asked. "You know, the one where you were going to explain what the fuck is going on? Maybe even tell us how the device is supposed to work?" She was starting to feel anxious. Why was it that when she finally felt like she was settling into who she was supposed to be, there was one more thing that made her different?

"Sorry." Rebecca cleared her throat. "Uh, right. According to Gregory, the Drude and the Valkyries are two sides of the same coin. That whole entropy thing? Well, the universe manifested the Valkyries as an answer to the Drude—the opposite, if you will. Your magics are opposed and cancel one another out. Same idea with how you exist in the universe. You're all energy, and a Drude is all body. You use a body to maintain the energy, and a Drude uses energy to maintain its body. The idea, at least according to Gregory, is that you would destroy each other, thus returning balance to the universe on its never-ending march of entropy."

"What does that have to do with my aura fading?"

"If a Drude loses all its magic, then all that's left is a body. There wouldn't be an aura left, like what I saw with you."

Mila narrowed her eyes in a deep frown. "Are you saying I'm like a Drude? I don't understand."

"I don't understand, either!" Rebecca threw her hands up in frustration. "That's why I said it was interesting."

CHAPTER FOUR

They all sat in stunned silence for a few seconds at Rebecca's sudden outburst before bursting into laughter.

"Okay, so I sort of understand how the device would work by that logic." Victoria drank some of her Lance special. "Our magics cancel each other out, so if we can flood him with celestial magic, it will burn up all his infernal magic and leave a body that we can kill. Without energy to rebuild the body, he would be truly dead."

Rebecca was nodding along as the Valkyrie spoke. "Exactly."

"No, not exactly." Mila couldn't believe the obvious flaw in their thinking. "Azoth *eats* Valkyries. Remember? That's kind of the problem. Why would he let all that celestial magic affect him when he could eat it, or whatever he does with it?"

"Ah, that's why you need the device. For a Drude to 'eat' celestial magic, or the power from a Valkyrie, in this case, he uses an ability to convert that power into infernal magic, but it takes some of his power to do it. It's a little like how a car needs spark plugs to make the fuel burn. He uses some of his magic to make all of your magic into something he can use and take into himself to increase his magic."

Victoria pursed her lips in thought. "If he can use his magic to get more magic from what we shove into him, how does that help us? Won't he simply convert it all and become more powerful?"

"That's why we need the device." Mila finally understood the theory Gregory had come up with all those years ago. "We've stored up hundreds of times more power than any individual Valkyrie can hold. I assume there's a limit to how fast Azoth can consume it. Remember, it took him a while to devour Heather—she had to be drained for days before she was weak enough for him to take."

"That's true," Victoria cut in. "When he took me captive, he didn't even try to devour me. He kept saying that he needed a Lone Valkyrie so that we would weaken one another. I may not be all that old in Valkyrie years, but I do hold more power than all but Missy in our small sisterhood. He must not have been fully recovered."

"Right. So, if he tries to take more than he can convert, then it will flood into him as celestial magic and start canceling out whatever power he's holding onto. With the sudden torrent of power rushing out of the device, it would quickly overwhelm his ability to convert it. It would be like trying to drink from a fire hose—you could never swallow fast enough not to get wet."

Rebecca made a playfully disgusted face. "That's a vivid but accurate analogy. Have you ever seen the movie *UHF*?"

Both women shook their heads.

"You should check it out. They play out this exact scenario on an insane children's show in that movie." She chuckled and shook her head as the scene from the movie played back in her mind. "God, that's a fucked-up movie. Funny, but fucked up."

"What's fucked up?" Finn walked out of the hallway, trailed by Danica. The elf wore a blue-and-white striped bikini. Her face was redder than an apple as she fought not to burst out laughing. She locked gazes with Mila, waiting for the reaction.

Mila felt her throat catch in terror at the sight of her lovably unaware dwarf. His chiseled and glistening body was on full display as he strutted toward the table full of women. It looked like he'd slathered himself in baby oil or some other tan-enhancing fluid, and could have easily fit into a body-building competition for hairy-chested lumberjacks. The only thing that was *technically* keeping him decent was the tiny black Speedo he'd picked up in Chincoteague. Mila was sure she'd hidden the tiny man panties in the back of a drawer in their closet, but one look at her nearly bursting best friend told her all she needed to know. Danica *had* packed the clothes, after all.

"You son of a bitch," Mila growled at Danica, who couldn't hold it in anymore and slapped her knee while she laughed like a hyena.

"Holy shit, Finn," Victoria said with a mix of horror and admiration. "You're not fucking around, are you? I think there's more material in my ankle sock than your swim trunks."

Finn gave her a sour look. "Not you, too," he said with

disappointment in his voice before raising his chin defi-antly. He snapped the waistband of the mini-trunks before continuing in a haughty voice, "I'll have you know these are perfectly reasonable and functional swimwear. I can't help it if you're too immature to see me as anything but a piece of meat."

"I'm so sorry," Mila pleaded, putting a mortified hand on Rebecca's arm. The look of slight confusion Rebecca wore reminded Mila of the first time she had seen Finn in the Speedo. She remembered how confused she had been at how he could stuff everything away in the straining pouch.

"What's wrong with his trunks?" Rebecca leaned in and quietly asked, as if she wasn't in on the joke but wanted to be.

"I mean, they're tiny," Mila waved a hand vaguely at his package, "and he's...not."

Rebecca narrowed her eyes and leaned in slightly as if she couldn't see what Mila was talking about. She turned back to Mila and raised an eyebrow. "Good for you?" She seemed to genuinely not understand the problem.

Mila opened her mouth to explain further, but her jaw snapped shut when she saw Lance strutting out of the hall-way, a pile of towels under one arm, and an identical Speedo barely covering his junk.

"Oh, God... I will never live this down, will I?" Mila muttered to herself as she watched the moment that would forever make it impossible for her to get rid of those ridiculous swim trunks.

Lance stopped ten feet behind Finn, his eyes going wide and a huge smile spreading on his face. "Oh, man! Twins!"

he shouted, thrusting out his hips and pointing to his trunks, then at Finn's.

Turning around, Finn saw Lance's excited face and his beard split into a matching smile. "Twins!"

The two men ran toward one another and pulled off a perfect leaping high five as if they'd been practicing it for years.

Danica fell to the floor, her legs no longer able to support her as her laughter sucked all the strength from her body. She held her stomach and wailed, tears running down her face. She would try to stop but then saw the two men spilling over with excitement, and it would start again.

Finn and Lance looked down at the incapacitated elf rolling back and forth.

"What's so funny?" Finn raised an eyebrow.

Danica calmed herself enough to point at Mila. "Her… Her face. Oh, my God. I can't… I can't breathe."

Finn and Lance looked over at Mila, their smiles returning. The two men put their fists on their hips and struck a wide stance. "Admit it, babe. We're twins. I told you these things were cool."

Mila felt the heat radiating off her face as she looked at the two men who could not look any less like twins if one of them was a squirrel. Finn was six-five and rippling with muscle with lightly tanned skin, where Lance was lucky if he were five-eight, had a farmer's tan, and was rocking the dad bod hardcore. She did have to admit that even if they weren't twins in appearance, they definitely were in confidence. She pressed her lips tightly together and nodded vigorously, adding a "Mhmm."

"Dad!" Grimm yelled, standing on the edge of the pool and waving his arms over his head. "Hurry up! I want you to throw me."

Lance smacked Finn on the chest with the back of his hand before taking off toward the pool. "Come on, you'll love this. I'm teaching Grimm how to do cannonballs."

Finn took off after him, acting more like a big kid than Mila had ever seen from the dwarf king. She had to smile as he winked at her on his way by. She lashed out with lightning-fast reflexes and smacked his ass as he passed.

"Love you, you big idiot," she shouted after him.

"Love you too, darlin'," he managed to get out before doing a rather impressive flip off the edge of the pool that turned into a cannonball, sending a splash of water all over the screaming and clapping Grimm.

Rebecca leaned in and shouldered Mila gently. "I know those trunks look ridiculous, but Lance loves them. Sometimes you have to let the people you love look like idiots because they like it. He loves the trunks, and I love him, so the trunks stay. In the end, what do I care?"

"Why were you acting like you didn't know what I was talking about? I thought I was going crazy."

Rebecca smiled. "Because I knew Lance would love the fact that Finn had the same trunks, and if I started laughing before he came out, I wouldn't be able to stop. Like I said, he loves those trunks. I didn't want to let him know that I've been lying about them for the last ten years. Besides, they're not all that bad. Look at that cute little tush! I want to pinch it."

Mila and Victoria laughed at the face Rebecca made while pinching her fingers together.

"Okay," Mila nodded, "I can admit, they do have a certain amount of appeal. I only wish they weren't so tight. They hide nothing."

"No… No they don't." Rebecca chuckled. "Why don't we change and join the fellas? I don't know about you, but I could use a little sunshine."

They all agreed, and Mila and Victoria headed for the spare room. Mila stopped to help Danica up off the floor, where she was still catching her breath.

"Did you pull a muscle or something?" Mila asked once Danica was on her feet.

The tall elf threw her long hair over her shoulder and checked that the top of the bikini was still in place. "Pretty close. Sorry, but I saw the trunks in a drawer and couldn't resist. Lance having the same trunks was the best coincidence on the planet."

Mila smiled. "It's fine. He's having fun. Besides, I like to see him in skimpy clothes. You're the one who's going to have to avoid looking him in the package all day."

Danica's face became slack while her eyes developed a thousand-yard stare as she realized what she'd done. Mila smiled and slapped her on the ass. "Good game, babe. You played yourself."

Heading for the hall where the spare rooms had appeared, Mila opened the first door on the left. She stepped in and nearly hit her head on the door as she tried to look anywhere but at Victoria, who was standing beside the bed completely naked as she untangled a burgundy monokini.

"Sorry, didn't realize you would be so naked so fast." Mila backed out the door.

"Get in here. What are you, some kind of prude? The bathing suits are in here, anyway," Victoria hissed in a whisper, motioning for Mila to come in and close the door.

Mila hesitated, but stepped into the room and closed the door behind her. "Why are you whispering?" Mila whispered as she took in the black and white modern room style.

Victoria pointed at one of the pillows on the bed. Mila saw a blue circle in the center of it. She shrugged indifferently, not understanding what Victoria was getting at until she realized it was Penny, curled into a ball and fast asleep. The faerie dragon slept so little in a given night that Mila had only seen her truly asleep a half-dozen times since they'd been living together. She would catnap, but she was never really asleep. It was more that she was conserving energy until her next snack.

An actual nap in the middle of the afternoon was unheard of.

"Is she okay?" Mila whispered, her voice thick with concern.

Victoria shrugged and reached out, letting her hand hover an inch above Penny's slowly rising and falling back. She held it there for a second or two before going back to untangling the many straps threaded through the complicated monokini.

"She doesn't have a fever." She finally got the garment the right way around and opened enough to step into it. "She's probably tired. She did spend all night reinforcing the wards on the condo. Wards are hard work. She'll come out when she wakes up."

Mila bit her lip and curled her toes into the thick-piled

carpet as she watched her friend sleeping. She hadn't realized Penny was up all night. Victoria was right—wards were hard work. Penny would join them in an hour or so.

Mila nodded at Victoria and smiled at Penny. "You're right, she's probably tired from this morning." She glanced over at Victoria and raised an eyebrow at the ridiculously sexy dark red monokini. The hips of the garment were nothing more than four evenly spaced straps holding the narrow front panel and even skimpier back panel snugly in place. The front covered her stomach with a six-inch strip of material that clung to her well-defined abs before widening to contain her breasts then narrowing to a choker collar she had to button closed. The back was a weave of a dozen straps that came down from the collar and laced across her shoulder blades, to attach to the front panel at the ribcage. The whole thing somehow covered more than the simple striped bikini Danica was wearing and yet was far more scandalous.

Cold dread settled in Mila's stomach. "Oh, God… What did she pick out for me? I swear to God, that girl pushes me too far sometimes. The sexy underwear I can handle. Finn loves them, and they make me feel sexy, but no one *knows* I'm wearing them. A bathing suit is completely different. *Everyone* will see that. If she picked that out for you… Fuck. It's like you poured sex appeal on yourself and let it dry into a garment."

Victoria looked at her with a questioning eyebrow before glancing down at the suit she was wearing and quietly chuckled. "Don't worry. Danica didn't pick this out for me. It's mine. I bought it a couple of days ago when Danica and I went shopping." Victoria smiled as she reached into the shoulder bag and brought out a handful of white and orange material. "She brought you two choices. That girl knows you quite well." She spread them out on the bed, revealing two *very* different choices.

"I would go with this one," the older Valkyrie whispered, pointing to the white suit and winking. She adjusted hers for a better fit and turned to check herself out in the full-length mirror on the wall, turned more to view her profile, then pivoted further and looked over her shoulder at her back. "Wow, this really does look like dried sex appeal. God, I've had this body for over a hundred years and I still forget how hot it is. I lucked out this time around." She gave her ass a light smack, not wanting to wake Penny.

"How do you do that?" Mila looked at her two choices.

"Do what?" Victoria turned and rested her ass on the built-in vanity between the two closets and crossed her arms.

Mila looked between the conservative orange one-piece suit and the white monokini of a more conservative design than Victoria's but still far sexier than Mila would have picked out. She picked up the white one and held it in front of herself. She liked the cut and knew she could rock it if she wore it. A regular old bikini was about the raciest she had ever gone, and that was only with close friends.

"I love this suit and I want to wear it, but there's something that won't let me. I get a feeling of dread in the pit of my stomach. I can't explain it."

Victoria pursed her lips and narrowed her eyes while looking Mila up and down. The stare went on for a while, each passing second making Mila a little more uncomfortable than the last. Eventually, the look made Mila bring her arms in and use the swimsuit as a kind of shield as she turned ever so slightly away from Victoria's intense stare. Finally, it was too much for Mila to take.

"What are you looking at?" she hissed angrily.

Victoria smiled. "Why did that make you uncomfortable?"

"Because you were looking at me weird."

"No." The ordinarily serious woman crossed her eyes and put on a stupid face. "This is looking at you weird."

Mila snorted a laugh and quickly covered her mouth, checking to be sure she hadn't disturbed Penny. "What the hell?"

"You weren't uncomfortable because I was looking at you. You were uncomfortable because of what you *thought* I was doing."

"And what did I think you were doing?"

"Objectifying you. You probably didn't consciously realize that was what made you uncomfortable, but you were reacting to being thought of as an object, not a person. Do you care if Finn stares at you?"

Finn watched Mila all the time, usually with a half-smile of contentment on his face. It didn't matter if she was loading the dishwasher, doing yoga, or taking a shower—he always wore the same blissful look. It wasn't like he was creeping on her, but she would catch him staring now and then. At first, it was a little weird, but after a while she enjoyed it. He loved her and couldn't help staring at her. She did the same thing to him, although she was a little slyer about it.

Mila smiled, recalling fond memories. "I like it when he watches me. It makes me feel special, I guess."

"What's the difference between him and a stranger staring at you?" Victoria pushed off the vanity and took the white bathing suit from Mila, then held it up to her body to see what it would look like on her.

"I suppose the difference is that he knows me."

Victoria rolled her eyes. "Well, that's obvious. But why does it matter?" She laid the suit on the bed and scooped up the orange one-piece, then tossed it into the shoulder bag.

"Because he knows there's more to me than my looks. I'm a Doctor of Anthropology, for crying out loud. I worked hard for that shit, and I don't want people to judge me only on the way I look." Mila's brows rose as she said it, and realized it was true.

Victoria smiled and gently rubbed the tops of Mila's arms in a motherly fashion. "There it is. It's an admirable thing to want people to judge others for who they are and not how they look. But here's the problem...it's never going to happen. Not with the way the world works now, anyway. But there is some good news." She smiled. "It doesn't matter what others think."

"I mean, it matters a little," Mila argued quietly.

"No, it doesn't. Not even a little bit." She sighed and crossed her arms again. "This is something you'll learn with time, and trust me, it's a hard lesson to understand fully, but you will. It might take you twenty years, or you could be a little more hard-headed like me and waste a couple of thousand years figuring it out. But in the end, you'll realize it doesn't matter one tiny little lick what other people think of you. You work to be the best possible person you can, and the rest will figure itself out. Trust me. It always works itself out."

"You can take that a little too far, though," Mila wasn't quite willing to write off everyone's opinions yet. "If you're an asshole and don't care about others, you're not going to have a good time."

Victoria laughed softly. "You're right on that one. I did say that you need to work to be the person you can be. If an asshole is the pinnacle of your evolution, then you won't make it very far. But, I don't think you're an asshole. Plus, we have a little advantage in that we never die. That's why I can say with absolute certainty that others' opinions of you don't matter." She pointed at the strappy white monokini. "Do you want to wear that?"

Mila laughed into her hand and sniffed, wiping at a little wetness at the corner of her eye, then nodded. "Yeah, I do. It's cute."

"It's not cute, dum-dum. It's sexy as fuck. But here's the real question. Let's see if you learned anything from the ancient knowledge I laid on you." She took Mila by the shoulders and looked her in the eye. "*Why* do you want to wear it?"

Mila bit her lip before answering. "Because I'll look cute, and Finn will love it."

"Sexy, not cute. And Finn would love it if you wore a used garbage bag. That guy is beyond in love with you. Why do *you* want to wear it?"

Mila frowned, thinking about all the reasons she would give herself not to wear the suit, and in the end, they all boiled down to what others would think of her. It made her a little sick to her stomach.

She looked up at her elder sister, a new determination burning in her eyes. There was a wash of freedom that spread through her as she began to drop all the baggage she hadn't known she was holding onto. She suddenly felt a hundred pounds lighter. It reminded her of the day she had cemented her conviction and finally released her magic's full potential.

"I want to wear it because I want to feel sexy. Because I'm not doing anyone harm by wearing it. Because what I wear doesn't define me. But most of all, because I want to. It doesn't matter what others think of me. I know who I am, and that's enough."

Victoria smiled and pulled her in for a hug. "I would have accepted 'because I want to,' but you said it better." She pulled back and held Mila at arms' length while she smiled down at her. "There's something about you that I can't explain." She shook her head and shrugged. "Get dressed. We have a pool to drink beside."

Victoria turned and headed for the door.

"Uh, Victoria?"

She turned with her hand on the doorknob. "What?"

Mila bit her cheek. "Can you show me how to put this thing on?"

Victoria chuckled and nodded.

CHAPTER FIVE

Mila felt a thrill at the look Finn gave her when she stepped out onto the deck and struck a pose. His dropped jaw and goofy smile stayed plastered on his face as pool water dripped from his beard. She heard a snort of laughter from Victoria standing behind her.

"You two are ridiculous," she said quietly to Mila's back.

"Yup. Wouldn't have it any other way."

Finn was sitting on the edge of the pool next to Danica with Grimm sitting between them, their feet in the water. Grimm was inspecting his and Danica's prosthetic arms. The little boy would stick his entire arm through the open weave of the dark yellow diamond material and tell Finn to move his fingers, then squeal with glee when Finn's fingers wiggled. Grimm would then turn to Danica and do the same thing with her forearm.

Danica looked up and smiled when she saw which suit Mila had chosen. She stuck her finger and thumb in her mouth and blew out a loud catcalling whistle along with a thumbs-up. Mila gave her a discreet middle finger and headed over to a row of lounge chairs right up against the edge of the far side of the pool where Rebecca and Lance were reclining, watching their son playing with Finn and Danica.

Mila was very aware of Finn watching her every step, the goofy smile still on his face. She took the recliner beside Rebecca, and Victoria took the one on the other side of Lance.

Rebecca was looking at her with a critical eye behind a pair of large black sunglasses. She was wearing a simple white bikini, somehow making it look more elegant than sexy.

"What?" Mila asked.

"You have to be the most beautiful dwarf in the universe. Finn's a lucky man."

Mila laughed. "I'm not a dwarf."

The witch gave her a knowing smile and laid back on the recliner. "You're mostly right, I suppose." She lifted her copper mug to her lips and finished off the drink. "Can you hand me the pitcher?" She pointed past Mila to a small fridge that hadn't been there when Mila sat.

"Where the hell did that come from?"

"We told you the house changes as needed." She reached down to the deck and rubbed one of the boards. "Who's a good boy? You are! Yes, you are."

Mila laughed and sat up, turning her back to Rebecca to reach the fridge, and grabbed a second copper mug from the little freezer for herself. She turned back to get Rebecca's mug and nearly jumped out of her skin when she found the woman leaning across her lounge chair, her face only inches from Mila's lower back. Rebecca looked up and met her gaze.

"You fucking liar. You said you weren't a dwarf." She smiled and pointed at Mila's Shield Maiden tattoo. "What's this, then?"

Mila took Rebecca's empty mug while laughing at her expression, and turned away to pour the drinks. "Finn gave it to me. Just because I have a dwarven tattoo doesn't make me a dwarf. It means…"

"Oh, I'm well aware of what it means. Are you aware that you're the only person in the universe who's *not* a dwarf and has that tattoo?" She took the filled mug from Mila and sat back in her recliner.

"It's only a tattoo."

"No, it's not." Victoria chimed in from where she laid back in her chair, her eyes closed and soaking up the sun.

Mila rolled her eyes. "Okay, I get it. It's a little odd," she looked across the pool at Finn as he jumped to his feet and in a flash, picked Grimm up and tossed him into the water as the little boy screamed in delight, "but it's only special because he gave it to me. It's not me. It's him." She smiled, then laughed when Finn didn't stop with Grimm. In a flash, he picked up a squealing Danica and tossed her in before jumping in himself.

"I thought dwarves didn't like water." Lance laughed along with the antics.

"He's fine with a pool since he can jump out if he needs to. It's the deep open waters he doesn't like. They keep him too far from his source of magic. That, and he doesn't float."

Finn shot out of the water, coming up under Grimm

and grabbing the boy as he passed, and tossing the little kid ten feet into the air. The two of them shouted with glee before splashing down, at the same time splashing water in Danica's face.

They watched the dwarf king play with the little witch boy and the stunning elf woman for half an hour before Finn peeled away, leaving Grimm with Danica. She held him in her arms and danced around in circles, sending splashing waves out with each revolution, both of them giggling loudly.

Mila watched Finn's dark shape skimming across the bottom of the pool and heading right for her lounge chair. She spun around onto her stomach so her face was right at the edge where he surfaced. She smiled at him as he wiped the water from his eyes with one hand.

"Hi," she said in a chipper voice.

He chuckled. "Hi."

"Are you having fun?"

"I am. It's nice not to be out hunting for treasure."

"I thought you liked hunting for buried pirate booty," she said through a wide smile.

"Oh, this is a setup for me to talk about your butt, isn't it?"

She laughed. "Maybe."

"Well, you do have a cute booty. Is that what you wanted to hear? Are you happy now?"

"Oh, my God. Get a room, you two. There are children present," Danica called from the other side of the pool.

"Just because you have super elf hearing doesn't mean that everyone can hear us, you know," Mila called across the water.

"Yes, we can," Victoria corrected, still reclined on her chair with her eyes closed.

Rebecca and Lance both nodded. "It's super gross," Lance added.

Mila and Finn started laughing. "Okay, we'll stop." Mila turned back to Finn. "Your booty is super cute in your little trunks."

"Oh, come on!" Danica shouted.

Mila looked over her shoulder and saw that Lance and Victoria were laughing, but she caught Rebecca staring at the tattoo on her back. They locked gazes, and Rebecca gave her another knowing smile.

"You guys ready to start grilling?" Finn asked.

Lance jumped up. "Hell, yeah. Let's do it. I'm starving."

"Luckily, Finn brought a whole cow's worth of filets." Victoria chuckled.

"Brought the good stuff, huh? I'm willing to forgive all the mushy talk for a good filet." Lance jogged over to a large outdoor kitchen setup with a built-in grill that could hold an entire cow and started lighting it.

"That wasn't there a minute ago, right?" Finn's brow furrowed.

"Good boy." Mila patted the concrete edge of the pool. She laughed at the concerned look Finn gave her and leaned in to kiss him. Out of the corner of her eye, she saw Rebecca looking at her tattoo with an amused smile on her face.

They cooked up a feast and drank more delicious mixed

drinks. As soon as the smells of cooking meat filled the house, Penny sauntered out and joined them for dinner. Mila's concern for her friend faded as Penny slowly woke up and joined in with her usual banter and impressive appetite. By the time they said their goodbyes, the sun was low on the horizon and Grimm was asleep on the couch, tuckered out from the long day of fun.

They all traded hugs and laughs while making plans to come back at the end of the week before Danica had to return to her regular work schedule.

They gathered in tight, and Danica formed a large bubble around them. Mila and Rebecca locked gazes. The witch smiled while looking from Mila up at Finn, who'd wrapped his arms around Mila and pulled her close to his abdomen, then back down at her.

Mila cocked her head and started to say something when the bubble popped and they were standing in the condo's dojo.

"Hey, boss."

They all turned to find Remmy standing on the couch, her feet and legs bare and obviously scrubbed clean. Her light green skin almost shined in the late evening sun that filtered in through the windows. On top, she only wore one of Finn's black t-shirts that hung down her tiny frame to her knees like a dress and showed off a fair amount of cleavage from the plunging V-neck. Behind her, the TV was on but muted and looked like it was showing one of the twenty-four-hour news channels. Mila couldn't figure out if the goblin was watching the news on mute, or if she had been surfing channels and happened to stop there. She still couldn't figure out why it was already on mute.

Victoria smiled and headed for the living room. "Hello, Remmy. You look rather clean tonight. Something special planned?" She came around the large L-shaped couch and plopped down next to the grinning goblin.

"Maybe later, but mostly because the boss told me to keep the furniture clean."

Finn sighed. "I meant that *if* you were dirty from hunting or whatever, then take a shower before you roll around on the couch. I didn't mean you had to shower every time you came over."

Remmy laughed. "I know that, boss man. I just came back from my shift at Christine's. I was all sweaty, and my leathers needed cleaning anyway, so I used the shower up here. The one in our condo is always packed, even after you installed the communal bath. Thanks for that, by the way."

"Oh, well in that case, thank you for remembering. And quit calling me boss man. You stopped calling Mila boss lady, why can't you do the same with me?"

The little goblin smiled mischievously. "Because Mila is my friend. You're my protector, and I'm your protector. Sorry, boss man. That's the way it works."

Mila had to lock her jaw so she didn't start laughing.

"But *we're* friends." Finn's brow furrowed with frustration.

Remmy shrugged. "Sorry, boss man. I don't make the rules."

Finn growled at the ceiling. "You made that rule up! No one else in your tribe calls me boss man but you."

"Not to your face. You told them not to so they stopped

until you're not around, then it's boss man this, and boss man that. It's like a mantra or something."

Now Mila was struggling to keep quiet. She felt her face turning red, but she didn't want to make it worse for Finn.

"If they don't call me boss man to my face, then why do you keep doing it?"

"Because I'm braver than them. I can face down your wrath, unlike those pansies."

The corner of Finn's eye twitched, and his cheek muscles flexed as he clenched his jaw. "I'm going to shower. Glad you could stop by, Remmy." He turned and marched into his and Mila's room.

As soon as the door closed, Mila snorted with a laugh. "Remmy! Why do you tease him so much? He's going to have an aneurysm one of these days if you keep it up."

"It's good for him." Danica laughed. She walked over to the couch and let Penny hop off her shoulder onto one of the back cushions before heading into the kitchen and pulling a bottle of water from the fridge. "It keeps him honest. Or something. Actually, it's simply amusing. Don't ever stop, Remmy."

The little goblin grinned and saluted Danica. "No problem, doctor lady."

Danica shot water out of her nose, and the rest of them cracked up with laughter.

"Did you only come over to take a shower and torment my boyfriend?" Mila grabbed a bottled water for herself.

"No, I came to deliver a message." She held up a blue stone that had been worn down to a concave button-like shape. "On my way home from Christine's, I ran into a lady in a big old cloak. She had the hood pulled way down and must have been using a spell to keep her face in shadows because I couldn't see a thing. She sounded like she had eaten a bag of gravel and forgot to swallow. Anyway, she seemed to know who I was and handed me this stone. She said to tell you that she wanted to meet with you, that you could pick the place and she would come to you."

"Why did she want to meet with me?" Mila came over and took the stone, inspecting it.

"Careful, she said to activate the stone, all you had to do was squeeze it between your fingers."

Mila quickly lifted her thumb from the divot in the center of the stone disk. "You should probably lead with that next time."

"Yeah, my bad. Anyway, she said that she wanted to help you kill Azoth. She also said that if you didn't come, then thousands of people would die."

Mila's eyes went wide. "She'll kill thousands of people if I don't meet with her?"

Remmy cocked her head and reconsidered what she'd said. "No, she said that if you didn't come then thousands of people would die, but I'm pretty sure she didn't mean she was going to kill them, more like she could help prevent it if you came. I don't know, the whole thing was shady and weird, but I thought I better tell you."

"Thanks." Mila flipped the stone over in her fingers a few times before looking up and seeing the news channel switch to a recording off someone's phone in Times Square. It showed a Jumbotron, and the woman on the screen sent a chill down Mila's spine.

"Turn that up!"

Remmy snatched the remote from the back of the couch and hit the mute button, returning the sound.

"Strange events in Times Square this evening. What was at first thought to be a terrorist message is now being dismissed as a practical joke of an odd persuasion," the voice-over said before cutting back to the beginning of the phone's recording, but this time it played the sound.

The video swung around to show that all the screens had the same image, before zooming in on one screen and holding relatively still.

The unmistakable image was of Missy standing in front of a blank white wall. Her long blue pigtails were gone, leaving a hack job of a haircut of blue tufts. It looked like she had cut it herself with a knife and no mirror. Her mouth worked back and forth for a few seconds, and Mila thought the volume had been muted again, but a low growling sound built until it was obvious that Missy wasn't talking, only making threatening animal noises at the camera.

The growling cut off and she started talking, her girlie voice lower than Mila remembered. "Listen up, bitch. I know you'll see this, so I'll only say it once. Azoth wants the Reaper. You bring it to him, and he doesn't start World War Three. Don't fuck around and try to get clever. Bring the Reaper, and he goes home. Otherwise, he'll take a million people and set them loose on the world. They will tear this ship apart to find your tiny ass. You want that blood on your hands? Three days. In three days, you bring the Reaper to the site of the first battle and this all goes away. Otherwise, he'll conjure a spell that will convert the innocent into a slathering mass of ghouls spreading their sickness across the world, and eating this ship from the inside out. The great *Earth* will crumble to dust, and his people will fall from the stars to scour the world clean."

By the end of the video, Missy was shouting, frothed spittle shooting from her mouth and hitting the camera's lens. She looked like a lunatic.

"What do you think, Kelly? An army of ghouls and spacemen? Sounds pretty credible to me," the handsome news man said as they cut back to him and a blonde woman.

The woman chuckled. "Sure does, Phil. In other bizarre news, a small town in northern Siberia has gone missing."

"The whole town?" Phil asked.

"The whol—

Remmy hit the mute button.

Mila swallowed hard and made eye contact with Victoria. "Well..." Mila sighed. "Shit."

CHAPTER SIX

"I guess we don't have to wonder what Azoth is up to anymore." Mila snuggled into Finn's body, his arm around her as they laid in bed. She held the small blue stone Remmy had passed to her, turning it over in her fingers. "Now we need to figure out who this belongs to."

Finn reached for the stone, and she handed it over. He held it up, scrutinizing the smooth button-like object a few inches from his face. "If I had to guess, I would say it's Yaminah."

Mila raised an eyebrow while watching him turn the stone over. "Why do you say that? Wouldn't her Geas keep her from helping?"

"Maybe. I've never heard of a Geas that couldn't eventually be overcome. They're a nasty bit of magic, but someone with the will and talent could circumvent the effects if given enough time." He reached over and set the stone on the side table before pulling Mila close and gently stroking his fingers over her forearm. "Back when I was in the military, curse-breaking was one of the required abilities to pass before graduating from boot camp. I get the feeling that Yaminah has the raw willpower to break out even if she doesn't have any formal training."

"I could see that. The first dream I had where Azoth took her, she seemed to be a pretty powerful mage. She's resourceful, too. That doesn't mean it's her, though. Missy is unbelievably powerful and she doesn't seem able to break free, and it sounded like she wanted to during our last battle."

"She might be powerful, but she doesn't sound all that mentally stable." Finn shrugged. "Mental fortitude is the backbone of curse-breaking. Missy is grieving the loss of her wife. Or at least, something similar to that."

"What if it's a play to get me alone? Let's say it is Yaminah. She could be setting me up so Azoth can capture me to get the Reaper."

"That's true, but she's not giving herself a great opportunity to grab you. You set up the place and time, and she didn't stipulate that you had to come alone or anything."

Mila snorted. "She wouldn't have to come alone, either. It could still be a trap."

"True," Finn shrugged into the pillow, "but why? If she grabs you and you don't have the Reaper on you, then what? I suppose they could try and make you talk, but they'd know that we would come after you, and with them holding you, we could find them in a few seconds with a good tracking spell. They could block it eventually, but all it would take is the second before they could get it up."

Mila slowly nodded as she thought it through. It didn't make a lot of sense for them to try and grab her. They would know that she wouldn't have the Reaper on her, and the risks to them would be fairly high for a low possibility of success.

"What if it's not Yaminah? Who would be the most likely candidate?" Mila tried to look at the situation from all angles.

She reached up and twirled her fingers through his chest hair while he pursed his lips in thought. "I don't know. It could be some random person who saw him and wants to help. I don't know why they wouldn't give Remmy the info, though." He shook his head. "No, I don't see how it could be anyone else. She was hiding her face, she knew Remmy on sight, and she handed over a fairly powerful enchanted stone. I think it's Yaminah."

"What are the odds that she wants to help?" Mila turned into him and kissed his chest.

"Fifty-fifty."

Mila giggled at a thought that crossed her mind. "We could wait until there's a thunderstorm and I could hit her with a lightning bolt again if she tries to betray us. I bet she's still pretty gun-shy."

Finn chuckled. "Speaking of... According to Victoria, you shouldn't be able to do that."

"What? Call down lightning? Why not? I'm a new Valkyrie. I thought the whole point was that we gained abilities to fit the situation."

"Yeah, I get that," Finn nodded, "but according to Victoria, that's a whole other power set from a Valkyrie. You guys can channel your power and create things with it, but manipulating the storms like that isn't something you should be able to do."

Mila bit her lip and furrowed her brow. "Well, what else

could it be? We know I'm a Valkyrie, so it has to be a Valkyrie ability. What else is there?"

Finn cleared his throat uncomfortably. "It could be a byproduct of the tattoo I gave you."

Mila pushed up so she was looking down into his face. "You want to run that by me again, big guy?"

"Calling down lightning is an ability that all Shield Maidens have," he said with a wooden smile. "Quite a few Dwarves have it as well. It has to do with our earth magic and how it interacts with the air. We change the polarity of the ground, and it makes the bolt discharge."

"I know how a lightning bolt works," she held up a hand, "but why didn't you mention this earlier? You know that Rebecca already thinks I'm a dwarf or something. Can you call down lightning, too?"

Finn chuckled and shook his head. "No, I never mastered it. Hell, I couldn't even get the hair on my arm to stand up. It's a pretty rare ability in my people."

"But all the Shield Maidens can do it?"

"Yes, but that's because the Emperor grants them the ability. Which I always found odd, since as far as I know the old man couldn't do it, either. But that doesn't mean anything here, because I'm not my father. I can't grant those kinds of powers. Even the title is only that, a title. Maybe your status as a new Valkyrie is feeding off the idea of the Shield Maidens?"

Mila raised an eyebrow and gave him a half-smile. "I'm not so sure anymore. Rebecca and Victoria have been quietly obsessed with the tattoo you gave me. What if there's more to it than simply a tattoo? I mean, I know it's magical by the fact that you used magic to make it, but what if there's more to it?"

He frowned slightly and pulled the sheets down, uncovering her lower back. "Lay down. I'll take a look."

Mila did so, curling her arms under her chest and turning her head away from him. She felt him sit up and pull the sheet down further to get a better look. She laid there in silence, hearing his deep and steady breaths as he inspected her. She let out a little sound of contentment when his fingers caressed the side of her hip before lightly slipping toward her spine. He traced the simple tattoo with the tip of a finger, making goosebumps appear on her arms and legs. A chill ran through her when his finger slipped lower down her ass cheek.

"Hmm. Looks pretty good to me," he said in a low baritone, his finger making a swirling motion on her butt cheek.

Her shoulders shook slightly as she fought the tickling feeling. "Are you talking about the tattoo or my butt?"

"Yes."

"I'm serious, here." She giggled. "Does it look different?"

"Nope. Toned as ever," he practically growled.

"The tattoo, Finn. Does the tattoo look the same?" She wanted to slap his hand away, but at the same time, she enjoyed the attention.

"Oh, right." His grin was evident in his voice. "It looks the same to me. Maybe a little brighter, but that could be because you're growing in power. Now, about this butt…"

Mila squealed as his hand cracked down on her exposed butt cheek. She launched herself up onto her knees and tackled him onto his back. He laughed as they bounced a few times on the bed, her ending up straddling him.

"Speaking of growing…" She waggled her eyebrows like Groucho Marx, even going as far as imitating chewing on a cigar.

Finn laughed and rested his hands on her hips. "Man, you've been extra frisky lately. What's going on with you? Not that I mind, it just seems a little sudden."

Mila shrugged and kicked the sheets off his legs. The comforter's folded weight at their feet and the momentum from the kick dragged everything over the edge to pile on the floor. She snorted a giggle, but quickly forgot about the covers as she turned back to him and leaned forward, her hands on his chest and arms locked.

"When I found out Valkyries can't have children, I stopped taking my birth control. Now that I'm off it, my hormones are returning to their college-day levels." She reached over his head and grabbed a hair tie off the side table. In one quick motion, she had her hair pulled back and secured in a messy bun.

"Damn, girl. You're putting your game face on really quick." His eyes grew wide.

"College levels, babe. Now, you might want to find something to hold onto."

"Um, am I going to have to install handles on the headboard?"

Mila gave him a slow shrug. "Wouldn't hurt."

"Daaaamn…"

CHAPTER SEVEN

Mila's eyes snapped open, and she sucked in a shallow breath as she went from deep sleep to wide awake in a heartbeat. She felt her skin flush with a clammy sweat that immediately evaporated and made her shiver into her pillow.

Blinking a few times to clear her eyes, Mila didn't move from her pillow. After a second or two, she awoke enough to realize that she could see just fine, but it was still dark in their bedroom. Her dark vision was kicking in though, and blurry movement caught her eye, making her hold her breath and try to focus.

Like a rubber band snapping back into shape after being stretched too far, Mila shifted to fully awake.

She carefully sat up, doing her best not to wake the lightly snoring Finn beside her. She peered down at her pillow and saw what had seemed like a blurry object, but was simply too close for her to focus on properly.

"Hello there," Mila whispered while leaning toward the large black-and-gold striped orb weaver. The three-inch-long spider was standing on her pillow, its four front legs waving back and forth in the air to get her attention. "Are you okay?"

The spider relaxed as if it had been trying to wake her for a while. A warning feeling entered Mila's mind. She had used her nature ability for long enough that she immediately recognized it as coming from the matron spider.

Mila furrowed her brow in concentration as she tucked her foot under her and leaned in further. She got the warning feeling again. Then she glimpsed an image from the spider's mind. At first, her brain couldn't make sense of the eight points of view from the multi-eyed creature, but she quickly adapted to the strange way of seeing.

It was an upside-down view of Larimer Street. The street itself had a few cars parked along it, but it was obviously late in the night. There seemed to be quite a bit of foot traffic, however. It was hard to tell if the people were drunk or if it was an effect of the spider's vision, but each person was stumbling up to windows and looking inside before moving to the next building.

"Are there people out there searching for something?"

The spider bounced up and down.

Mila's eyes widened a little. "How long ago was this?"

The spider pointed a black-and-gold arm to the window. "*Now.*"

Mila nodded. "Okay, thank you. I'll check it out." She looked over her shoulder at Finn's sleeping form. "Uh, try not to wake him. He might not be so careful upon finding you in his face."

The orb weaver gave her a two-legged salute, then pulled herself up on a thread of webbing Mila had missed in the dark. After a complicated series of swings, the large spider was at the window and crawling through a hole in the screen Mila had left for such an occasion.

Carefully stepping out of the bed, Mila found Finn's discarded black t-shirt on the floor and quickly pulled it over her head. The shirt came to her knees and past her elbows despite it being short-sleeved. She carefully opened the door out to the dojo and checked that Finn was still sleeping before pulling the door closed until there was only a crack remaining. She didn't want to have to open it again and chance waking Finn up when she returned.

Walking across the blue mats of the large open practice area, Mila headed toward the living room and the French doors that led out onto the wraparound balcony.

When she reached the back of the couch, Mila froze when she saw Victoria sleeping there. Her sleeping on the couch would have been weird enough since she had a guest room, but the fact that Remmy was sprawled out on top of her made Mila do a double-take.

The two of them were under a blanket, but it was fairly obvious that Remmy didn't have a top on, and leaning to the side a little verified that Victoria didn't, either.

"What the fuck?" Mila whispered, trying to make sense of what she was seeing as anything other than what it looked like.

Her brain was rebelling at the idea of the powerful CEO sleeping with the four-foot-tall goblin. Not that Remmy wasn't attractive, quite the opposite, but she was still two feet shorter than Victoria... Actually, Mila guessed she and Finn were about as mismatched as Victoria and Remmy. At least size-wise.

Mila shook her head and decided it was something she would have to ask Victoria about later. Maybe she should ask Remmy. That way, she would be sure to get the truth. There was no such thing as double-speak for Remmy. It was all truth, all the time. Usually to a graphic degree.

Moving to the double doors to the balcony, Mila quietly opened them and stepped out into the cool night air. She leaned on the railing and peered down into the street, trying to make sense of what the spider had shown her.

As in the vision from the arachnid, there were a good dozen people milling about the street. Now that she saw them with her eyes, she was convinced they were drunk. Their walks were a little too shuffling, and they tended to run into things before bouncing off and stumbling in a new direction. Something about them gave Mila the chills, though. There was something about the scene that wasn't adding up.

"They're not walking together," Mila muttered, finally figuring out what was off.

Drunk people clumped together. These people were out on their own, and unlike drunks, they stopped at every window they came to and stared into the buildings before moving on to the next.

Something else didn't seem right as she looked up and down the street. There weren't any cars driving down it. She saw headlights a few blocks away, but all the vehicles turned off before they got to within three blocks of her condo. When she walked around the corner, it was the same on 21st Street. The same wandering zombie-like people peering into windows and no cars driving closer than a few blocks.

Denver was a fairly large city, and like all large cities it never entirely went to sleep. Mila couldn't remember the last time there wasn't a car passing on the street below.

Zombie-like... Mila's eyes went wide. Not zombie-like, thralls. Those were thralls down there, and they were searching for the condo. Yaminah knew she lived somewhere near the Market, but evidently not an exact location.

Tightness in Mila's chest cut off her breath. What if the thralls found them? There were more people living in the building than Mila and Finn. There were the goblins, the Selkie twins staying in the small unit on the second floor, and an orc family that Finn had brought home a few weeks ago while they got themselves back on their feet. Rising panic built in Mila as she tried to figure out the best way to warn everyone while at the same time trying to figure out where to take them all. She guessed they could probably go to Christine's in a pinch, but they would still—

A small purple rune glowing at the base of the railing caught Mila's attention, and she relaxed. Penny had already thought of all this. Mila ran through the protections Penny had placed on the building.

She had called it an observation rune. If Mila was remembering right, it made it so that anyone planning to cause harm to an inhabitant simply wouldn't see the building when they came looking.

Mila made a note to kiss that little blue devil on the lips the next time she saw her. Which made her wonder how Penny was feeling.

Mila followed the edge of the balcony as she tried to get a good count of thralls searching the surrounding buildings. She was up to sixteen when she came to the end of the railing that stopped at the back of the building and overlooked the back alley where the garages were. She looked down to see if any of the thralls were back there and froze.

Missy stomped down the center of the one-lane road, her loud footfalls sending up splashes of water that ran down the center of the alleyway. Her chopped hair didn't look any better than it had on her broadcast in Times Square. She held her silver sword in one hand while the other held a small flame for light. Black infernal magic tinged the fire and sent odd anti-shadows dancing along the walls.

Low-volume mumbling rose from the obviously frustrated fallen Valkyrie, but Mila couldn't make anything out. The closer Missy got, the brighter the rune at the base of the railing became, but it didn't seem to be in any danger of overloading. At least, not yet.

"Well, fuck me." Mila suddenly felt under-dressed and under-armed. "This could be really bad."

CHAPTER EIGHT

Arms snaked around Mila from behind, making her yelp in fright.

"Whoa. Sorry, babe," Finn said close to her ear. "Didn't mean to scare you. What are you doing out here?"

"Fucking hell, Finn. You scared the shit out of me," Mila gasped while pointing over the balcony's railing. "A little spider let me know we had a visitor."

Finn leaned forward to look down into the alley over Mila's shoulder. She felt his arms stiffen around her. "Missy? How the hell did she find us?"

"I don't think she has." Mila toed the glowing rune at the base of the railing. "Pretty sure Penny's wards are doing their job. There are thralls all up and down Larimer and 21st. I think they're searching the area. Yaminah knew I live close to the Market, but she didn't get a chance to follow me home."

Finn stepped away and Mila saw that he wore only a pair of red boxer briefs as he leaned against the railing beside them and peered down into the street.

"Where are all the cars?" Finn quietly asked before looking further down the street to see headlights turning off to detour around the area. He frowned, checked the other direction and saw the same thing. "She must have put up a compulsion spell to keep the area clear. I bet most of the buildings have emptied out as well. Something strong enough to deter drunks has to be a piece of powerful magic."

"Why aren't we affected? Wouldn't we feel it?" Mila stepped up next to him and wrapped herself around his arm for warmth. The night chill was getting to her as it cut through the thin t-shirt. It seemed she wasn't entirely dwarf—if she was at all.

Finn nodded toward one of the glowing runes. "Because Penny's a badass." He chuckled. "It's not the first time she's saved my ass with some of her patented forethought." He pressed his lips together and took in the wandering masses before looking over the back railing to see that Missy had come closer, but still seemed unaware of the entire building. "We need to lead them away. I've granted far too many people sanctuary here to let them be attacked. Penny's runes are good, but no rune is perfect. They're already blazing pretty bright."

"I was thinking the same thing," Mila confessed. "I didn't want to go out there and chance being seen by our neighbors."

"I don't think there's much threat of that happening. The spell she has over the area will take care of any onlookers before they become a problem."

Mila smirked. "I guess this blows the theory that our mystery woman is Yaminah."

"Why do you say that?" Finn looked at her with a questioning eyebrow.

Mila waved a hand at Missy walking closer. "Because Yaminah was the only one who knew where we were. She obviously told Missy. That doesn't sound like the actions of someone who wants to help us."

Finn snorted a laugh. "I suppose so, but that doesn't mean it's not Yaminah. She could have told them back when her Geas was still active."

"You don't know that she broke free of her Geas. I don't think she's our girl."

"I don't know. It makes too much sense. She hates Azoth. She's powerful. I'm pretty sure she hates Missy too, from the things you said. She's my guess." He gave her a sly half-smile. "I'll bet you it's her. If it is, we install those handholds in the headboard."

Mila snorted a laugh much louder than she intended and thanked Penny for the silencing wards. "So, now we're going to see this mystery woman?"

Finn shrugged and looked down at the street filled with thralls. "I think we could use every advantage we can get. They're practically knocking on the front door. We have too many innocents here for them to bring the fight to us."

Mila nodded against his arm. "I agree. We need to take care of this."

"Take care of what?" Victoria stepped out onto the balcony, the blanket wrapped around her shoulders like a priest's robe.

"Victoria," Mila stepped away from Finn, "we have a situation." She gestured out at the thralls.

It took Victoria a few moments to understand the

implications of stumbling people wandering the street, but her face soon widened in shock. "They found us?" She leaned over the rail and scrutinized the people as she walked closer to the alley. "They won't be alone." Her emotions bubbled up. "Someone has to control them. Have you seen Azoth or—" her jaw clicked shut when she spotted Missy stomping down the alley.

Mila felt heat radiate off Victoria before she saw any sign that the older Valkyrie was doing anything out of the ordinary. By the time Mila realized that Victoria's anger was getting the better of her, it was too late.

A feral growl rumbled from deep within the tall blonde woman as the blanket fell from her shoulders, exposing her naked body. Her skin glowed with golden light seconds before her power surged forth with a roar of anger and hurt. Fists clenched, Victoria flexed her muscled back and wings of golden light exploded from her, the stylized feathers spreading up and out like a bird of prey flexing before the attack. The wings weren't connected to her back or made of anything solid, but they were an impressive show of her power.

The rune at Victoria's feet sparked, then sent up a blue flame before crumbling to black soot that vanished into the wind. Mila saw the other runes along the balcony glowing brighter than seemed safe, sending up eerie shadows along the walls.

"I will rip her goddamned face off," Victoria growled while reaching for the railing.

Mila saw Missy's demeanor change in an instant. She went from frustrated to focused and began searching the area with narrowed eyes.

Mila stepped forward at the same time Finn did and they both grabbed one of the enraged Valkyrie's arms, pulling her back and putting themselves between her and the railing.

Victoria's eyes glowed with golden energy as she snarled at the two of them blocking her way. "Move. I will have my revenge for my sisters."

Mila felt dread deep in her core. This was a woman who had lived longer than any empire on *Earth*. She was trained to be a warrior against enemies that could rip the human race to shreds. She was power incarnate. Mila's body wanted to shrink away from that power. It wanted to apologize and let her elder pass. She couldn't stop Victoria if she tried.

Mila felt a spark snap her in the lower back a breath before Finn gently touched her with light fingertips. The zap made her breath catch in her throat, and her eyes widened in shock. Power flowed from his hand into her. It wasn't like he was giving her magical power—this was something different, something more than magic.

Suddenly, the growling powerhouse of a woman standing in front of Mila wasn't frightening at all. She was an impetuous and reckless child who needed to be dealt with.

Mila's eyes narrowed, and she stepped right up into Victoria's personal space. The blonde woman was a good foot taller than her, but Mila didn't care. She pressed a finger into Victoria's chest and pushed the surprised woman back a step.

"You will do nothing of the sort. You don't have the right to take revenge at the cost of the innocents living in this building. Those people are protected by Finn and me, and if you do anything to bring harm to them, then you're bringing our wrath down upon you."

Victoria's expression changed from pure rage to wide-eyed surprise as she stumbled back a step. The light of magical power faded from her eyes.

"Those fallen Valkyries are not *your* sisters. They were *our* sisters. You are putting us and the rest of the inhabitants of this building in danger by lashing out like a child. You're smarter than that, Victoria, and I'm ashamed that you don't know how to control yourself." Mila stabbed her finger into Victoria's chest again, this time making the Valkyrie wince in pain. "You will stand down and stop this petulance. We'll take care of Missy and her thralls, but we'll do it in a way that doesn't put us all in danger. Is that understood?"

Victoria's wings faded to motes of golden light that faded from existence as they floated away on the breeze. She swallowed, her wide eyes locked onto Mila's. "I... I understand." She swallowed again before looking down in shame. "I'm sorry."

Mila reached up and lifted her chin so that she was looking at her once again. "I understand your anger. Betrayal is the most vicious of attacks. But you have to think about those around you."

Victoria nodded, her eyes glassy with tears. "I'm sorry. I do know better. Thank you."

"I know you're here somewhere, bitch!" Missy called up from the alley, the insanity making the inflection of her words sound off, as if she were emphasizing the wrong syllables.

Mila patted Victoria's arm, then stepped to the railing. The blue-haired woman was waving her silver sword around her head as she slowly spun in a circle looking up at random buildings.

"If you don't show yourself in the next five minutes, I'm going to have my thralls start tearing into buildings at random. They'll kill everyone they come across until we find you." She held up her wrist and pointed at the watch on it. "Look here! I even have a timer." She clicked the button, making the watch beep. "Five minutes. And for fuck's sake, bring the Reaper."

Missy smiled, showing far more teeth than she should as she walked out of the alley and into the street, swinging her sword like a bat at a parked car. Sparks shot up as the sword sliced through steel and glass like it wasn't even there.

"Uh, is everything okay?" Remmy stepped out onto the balcony, surprisingly wearing the t-shirt that Victoria had been wearing earlier. Mila had figured the little goblin would be naked as usual.

Tossing the discarded blanket to Victoria, she and Finn headed back inside. "Missy's here. Finn and I are going to take care of it."

Remmy's brows rose up her forehead. "What do you want me to do?"

Mila looked over her shoulder at Victoria following them inside and hiked a thumb at her. "Keep Victoria inside. She's going to sit this one out."

Victoria opened her mouth to protest but snapped it shut at a look from Mila and nodded. Her face was still dark and clouded with anger, but she seemed to understand that she was too emotional for the delicate situation right now.

"You guys fighting in your skivvies, boss man?"

Finn chuckled. "Wouldn't be the first time, but no. We need to gear up."

Remmy nodded as she led Victoria back to the couch and pushed her onto it. "Probably for the best. It's no good fighting with your dangly bits hanging out."

CHAPTER NINE

Mila and Finn stepped out onto the roof of the condo through the stairwell door. The city was laid out in front of them, sparkling in the moonless night.

They had changed into their battle gear. Finn wore a pair of jeans and a black t-shirt with his brown leather harness over his shoulders, and Mila a gray V-neck and the black leather pants and moto jacket she had picked up with Remmy in San Francisco along with her corset holding Gram and the Ivar pistol.

Stepping to the edge of the roof, Mila looked down and saw that Missy had taken up a position in the middle of Larimer Street, her sword held to her side as she watched her wrist.

"Two minutes!" Missy called, a look of glee on her face.

"How are we doing this?" Finn planted a foot on the short wall at the edge of the roof.

Mila glanced up and down the street, trying to see the battle as it would unfold. Missy stood at one end, with her thralls all having moved past her in their systematic but fruitless search.

"Can you handle the thralls by yourself?" Mila already knew the answer.

Finn snorted, a half-smile on his face as he looked her way. "Are you serious?"

She smiled. "Just making sure. Okay, I'll head over that way and come up behind Missy. I'll get her to turn around and put her back to the thralls. You climb down the fire escape, and as soon as her back is turned, you take them out. She probably won't expect you to be here, so hopefully we can take her without much of a fight."

"Are we killing her or taking her captive?"

Mila bit her lip and considered the pros and cons. "In the end, she's a victim, even if she did kinda start this whole thing. I would like to save her if we can. I think once Azoth is gone she might recover." She frowned. "Eventually."

Finn nodded in agreement. "Plus, we might get some information from her. We still don't know what Azoth is planning."

"True. Information is our friend at this point, regardless of where we get it from." Mila looked over at Finn with a thin-lipped frown. "That said, if we need to, don't hesitate to take her out. I would like to save her, but not at the cost of more lives. She chose to do this even if she didn't realize it would get this bad."

He nodded. "How are you going to get over there? I don't think you can sneak two blocks with all those thralls down there."

Mila pulled the hem of her moto jacket down as she stood as tall as she could. "I think it's about time I learned how this whole flying thing works."

"You think you can figure it out in a minute and a half?" Finn headed for the fire escape.

"I've been working it out in my head. I have an idea of how to do it." She smiled at him. "No time like the present to learn."

He winked and swung his leg over the ladder. "I believe in you, darlin'."

"I know you do," she replied before he slid down the iron ladder with a smile. She blew out a breath and looked out over the skyline. "Now, I have to believe in myself."

Mila closed her eyes and felt for the power that was always churning in her core. It was warm and lively, making her feel strong and alive like nothing she had ever experienced before coming to know what magic was.

She had talked the process over with Victoria on several occasions, but there was always some excuse for why it wasn't time to try it. Victoria had drilled the method into her, and to be truthful, it sounded almost too easy. Mila knew she could do it. She'd levitated a little while she was practicing in the shower the other day.

The truth was that Mila wasn't a huge fan of heights. It was silly when she thought about it. It wasn't like she was afraid of falling—she would be using her power to hold herself up, and she trusted herself. It would be like flying in an airplane. She was fine with that. True, the takeoff always made her a little queasy, but once she was up in the air she was okay. This would be like that.

Focusing her power into herself, similar to the way she made herself stronger and quicker, she thought about where she wanted to go. She felt herself become lighter, but a spurt of panic dropped her back to the loose stone covering the roof. She drew a breath and started over. This time, she opened her eyes and focused on where she wanted to go. Her legs flexed awkwardly as crackling power surrounded her and lifted her a foot off the roof.

"Okay, you got this, Mila," she muttered, trying to psych herself up. "It's only a quick little shot. Out and around—don't let her see where you came from. Just a quick shot of power. You got this."

"One minute!" Missy yelled into the oddly silent portion of the city.

Mila clenched her jaw. There was no time to fuck around. She let the power flow into her, and it launched her across the roof and out into the open.

She wanted to scream. She wanted to close her eyes. She wanted to land and never try this again. What she did instead was focus on all the people living in the condo building—people she now thought of as family—and swallowed her fear in one big lump, forcing it down into a corner of herself that was good at holding onto the things she didn't like to think about. She stuffed it between her fear of being alone and her fear of public speaking, shelving it to collect dust until the day she faded from the universe.

It probably wasn't the healthiest way to deal with it, but she didn't care. She didn't have time to talk it out with a therapist. She had a world to save.

The wind rushed past Mila's face, making her eyes water as the city blurred below her. When she was a good mile out, which happened far faster than she thought possible, she changed direction, curving up and over and coming around to Larimar Street from an odd angle to the condo. She was several hundred feet in the air and coming back down at breakneck speed when she spotted Missy still staring at her watch.

The ground came up fast, and Mila used her magic to bolster her body and muscles, unsure of how to land properly. She kind of cut off the power and the golden buzzing field around her snapped out of existence, leaving her in free-fall for the last thirty feet or so. Her stomach came up into her throat, but she swallowed it and aimed her feet for the center of the road about twenty feet behind Missy.

"Tim—" Missy's shout cut off as Mila slammed into the pavement, blasting a small crater from the semi-soft tarmac.

Mila flexed her legs and dropped to one knee as she put out a hand to keep herself from face-planting. Mila almost laughed when she realized she'd landed in the classic superhero three-point stance. She may as well milk it.

Missy spun around, her wide-mouthed smile looking more demonic than anything. Mila waited for her to take in the small crater and her stance before slowly rising to her feet and locking a hard stare onto the Dark Valkyrie.

Missy raised an eyebrow while looking Mila over. "A little dramatic, don't you think? If you're not careful, you'll hurt yourself with those sorts of antics."

Mila smirked while casually reaching back and pulling

Gram free. She whispered the power word, and the golden sword unfolded with a series of quiet clicks. "Coming here alone is a good way to get yourself hurt as well."

The dull ache in Mila's knees was a telltale sign that Missy was right, but Mila wasn't about to admit that.

Missy laughed—really laughed, throwing her head back and holding her stomach and everything. Mila found it a little obnoxious, even if Missy was crazy.

"Haven't you figured it out yet, child? You weren't my equal before I took the infernal taint. Now?" She chuckled again. "Well, now it's not fair to you."

"Maybe." Mila casually shrugged. "But that's a pissing contest I don't need to concern myself with quite yet."

"Oh, isn't it? How do you—"

"I thought I had three days," Mila interrupted, making Missy's face darken with anger.

"Azoth gave you three days as a deadline. That doesn't mean he doesn't want it sooner. If I can retrieve the Reaper before the deadline, then I get a reward."

Mila snorted. "Like what? A box of candy? A toy car? A clue?"

"I get what I wanted all along—a way home. I bring him the Reaper before the three days are up, and he takes me to my Jennifer right then and there." Her crazed look fell away for a moment as she stared off into the ancient past. That look of painful longing was almost enough for Mila to understand why Missy had done it all.

Mila thought about the lengths she would go to return to Finn if they had become separated. She could almost see herself going as far as Missy had, but Mila knew there was one thing that would always stop her from going too far.

"Would Jennifer approve of the things you've done to return to her?" Mila knew what Finn would say if it were her.

Missy's face fell, then turned to anger in a smoldering flash as she locked her gaze on Mila once again. "You don't have a clue what it's like. How dare you talk to me as if you could even begin to understand the love Jenny and I have?" She took a step forward, her empty hand beginning to glow with gold and dark purple magic.

"I want to help you, Missy. When I defeat Azoth, I can free you of his taint on your soul. You can be free once again," Mila pleaded but stood her ground.

Tears sprang to Missy's eyes, and she fought to keep them at bay as she continued to advance. "You can't defeat him. I didn't stand a chance against him. He'll crush you beneath his heel without thinking twice. There is no escape from a Drude. Only pain and servitude. My only option is to believe that he will set me free when I fulfill my end of the bargain."

"That's not going to happen. You know he won't ever set you free."

Missy swallowed. "I have to hope. It's all I have." She looked Mila over as if for the first time, her eyes growing wide. "Where is it? Where's the Reaper? I told you to bring it!"

Mila felt sorry for this broken woman. She didn't deserve what was being done to her. Then again, she started this intending to free her mortal enemy, so maybe she was getting what she deserved.

Mila sighed. "I didn't bring it, Missy. Why would I hand

it over when it's the only thing keeping the Drude in check?"

The sorrow instantly vanished from Missy's face. "You stupid child. I'm going to enjoy tearing you limb from limb. Thralls, attack!" she screamed, pointing her sword at Mila's chest.

CHAPTER TEN

Mila raised an amused eyebrow while staring Missy down. The woman was slowly starting to realize that her minions weren't attacking as she'd ordered.

The Valkyrie frowned, her expression more angry than confused. "I said attack, you worthless husks!" she screamed, spinning around to see what the holdup was.

Mila heard the click of Missy's teeth as her jaw snapped shut and she sucked in a breath.

Arrayed down the street were two dozen stone spikes fifteen to twenty feet long. They were two feet in diameter at the base and tapered to a needle's point. The long shafts stuck out at odd angles, creating a chaotic latticework filling the valley between buildings on either side of the street. Halfway up each of the spikes was an impaled thrall. Every one of them was limp and obviously dead.

Walking through that gruesome forest directly toward the two Valkyries was a dour-faced Finn. His right hand glowed with purple dwarven magic. As they watched, the spikes silently sucked themselves back into the asphalt at such great speed that the dead thralls hung in the air for a beat before they rained down onto the pavement with hollow, wet thumps.

Missy turned back to Mila, her rage burning with new fury. The two women stared at one another for a beat before Missy charged in while raising her sword for a killing blow.

Magic flowed through Mila in a flash, bolstering her body to heroic levels as she brought Gram up in a defensive posture. The two swords clashed, sending a shower of golden sparks into the night air. Missy slid her sword off Gram at an angle, grinding more sparks from the two blades before she spun around, whipping her weapon in a wide arc to smash into Gram once again as Mila moved to block.

Gritting her teeth, Mila pushed back against Missy's weight, making the taller but thinner woman have to dance backward or be slashed across the chest when the two swords slid apart.

Before Mila could reset for an attack, Missy was already on her again, this time coming at her with a one-handed overhead chopping motion. Mila dropped to one knee, getting Gram up barely in time for the weapons to ring out like a bell.

A glowing orb of black and gold shot from Missy's free hand, only inches from Mila's face. Mila pivoted on her knee with a speed she would have thought impossible only a few weeks ago and dodged out of the orb's sizzling path.

The magic sphere slammed into the road, sending molten asphalt splashing into the air and raining down in a wide fan-shape for thirty feet.

Pulling Gram back, Mila held out her forearm and formed a translucent golden shield. With her other hand, she made a claw and focused raw celestial power into it. A ball of light so bright it hurt Mila's eyes formed between her fingers before shooting out and slamming into the ground at Missy's feet.

The asphalt exploded upward like with Missy's orb. However, Mila's attack blasted Missy into the air as well. Mila used the shield to protect herself from the point-blank attack, but the force of the blast sent her to her ass, where she dismissed the shield so she didn't cut herself with the razor-sharp Gram.

Missy tumbled backward, a snarling scream escaping her lips. She was spinning head over feet, molten bits of tarmac sizzling into her clothes and skin.

Golden light instantly formed around the fallen Valkyrie and she shot forward, her sword pointed at Mila's throat.

While bringing Gram up to block the diving blow, Mila realized she wasn't going to get her defenses up in time. A pillar of rock shot up from under Missy in mid-flight, slamming into her stomach like a stone fist. The blow practically folded her in two as her momentum instantly changed from forward to upward. Mila heard the gush of air from Missy's open mouth.

Finn gave Mila a questioning nod as the purple magic faded from his hand. Mila nodded back, noticing that a flood of thralls was pouring in from the side streets and alleys. Finn turned, his jaw setting and Fragar flashing in the streetlights as her dwarf charged the closest group.

Not having any time to admire Finn doing what he did

best, Mila scrambled to her feet barely in time to get a shield up and block another diving charge from Missy, who now had blood trickling from the corner of her mouth. Taking the opportunity to finally strike, Mila swung Gram up around her shield, aiming for the exposed torso between Missy's short skirt and cropped top.

Golden sparks exploded from where Gram slammed into Missy's hastily erected shield.

The next thing Mila knew, she and Missy were tumbling across the street in a tangle of arms, shields, and swords since Missy hadn't slowed her dive into Mila in the least. Pain exploded in Mila's right thigh as her knee struck the curb, and the impact finally threw the two women apart.

Mila tried to stand, but her knee wouldn't take her weight and she fell back down, which turned out to be a blessing in disguise as Missy's sword whistled through the air where her neck would have been.

Growling like a wild animal, the older but younger-looking Valkyrie kicked out with one of her high platform combat boots, aiming for Mila's face.

Mila dropped her shoulder and rolled to the side while reaching behind her back with her free hand. Coming back up onto her knee as it burned with pain, she pointed the Ivar at Missy's exposed side and pulled the trigger.

A lance of pure celestial power shot out at point-blank range and slammed into Missy's shield arm. The golden translucent barrier blocked most of the shot, but the core of the bolt drove a hole in the shield and slammed into Missy's exposed side.

There was a flash of blinding light, and Mila threw up

her shield to protect herself from the blowback as Missy was once again launched backward into the street.

"Finn!" Mila shouted, judging where the flailing Missy would land. Finn chopped a thrall in half, its upper body sliding to the ground as the legs took one last step before collapsing. He turned and saw Missy headed his way and smiled with that evil grin he got in the heat of his berserker's rage. "Don't kill her!"

He gave a reluctant nod and turned Fragar so he would strike with the flat of the blade. Missy realized what was happening a split second too late as she looked up and saw Finn stepping into a two-handed swing with his axe.

A hollow gong sound rang up and down the street as the runed axe blade smashed into the side of Missy's head. Her body went limp and tumbled to the side, rolling for a good fifteen feet before stopping, her eyes closed and arms twisted around her limp form in an uncomfortable-looking position.

Mila blinked in silent surprise at how well it had played out. She had been trying to line up the shot to do exactly what she had but was impressed that she'd pulled it off.

Finn spun back around to face the still-advancing horde of thralls, but the soulless beings shuffled to a stop and looked around with blank stares.

"What the fuck?" Finn stood from his crouched attack position and cocked his head to the side.

Then black void portals opened behind each of the remaining thralls, and they stepped backward into them before they all winked out in quick succession.

"What the fuck?" Finn echoed himself, but this time with a little more force.

Mila tried to stand, but her knee screamed, and she fell onto her ass. She reached down and felt her knee through the supple leather pants, which had already healed themselves back into perfect condition although she'd seen the large hole in the knee from the impact.

She sucked in a breath as she felt the split in her kneecap. Holding back a screaming sob of agony, Mila felt the normally hard bone flex down a central crack and open like a split fruit.

Closing her eyes, and feeling a tear of pain roll down her cheek, she channeled her power into the bone, flooding the area with healing magic.

The move drained her power reserves severely as the bone knitted together, but she didn't care. If it took everything she had, she would do it to make the pain stop. She had never realized how sensitive a knee could be.

After what felt like an eternity, the pain faded away and a numb buzzing feeling that sent pins and needles down her calf and into her foot replaced it.

"You okay?" Finn squatted in front of her.

She nodded and wiped the tear away with the back of her hand. She noticed that he'd broken his rage and was coming down from his high as the battle lust drained away. "Broke my kneecap. I already took care of it." She folded Gram down and clicked it and the Ivar back into the holster at the small of her back before holding her hands out to him. "Help me up. My leg's asleep."

"I don't think I'll ever get over the idea that you can heal yourself. That's not a common thing, F.Y.I." He pulled her to her feet with no effort on his part.

"F.Y.I.? Well, look at you finally getting the lingo down."

She laughed while using his arm for support as she tested out the still-numb leg.

"I'm a quick study."

She gave him a doubtful smile. "You've been here for nearly a year. I don't know that I would call that fast."

"When you live for a couple of hundred years, nine months is pretty fast."

"Is that all it's been? Nine months? That can't be right." Wonder made her eyes larger than usual as she looked up at him.

"Just about," he confirmed while looking at the mess in the street. "We need to do something about this. That spell she put up won't last forever, and I don't think people will ignore a couple of dozen chopped-up bodies in the road."

The numb tingling had finally faded, and Mila felt comfortable taking her weight. She stomped her foot a few times and didn't feel any pain in her knee, so she marked it down as a win. When she glanced up, she saw what he was talking about. The scene was gory, to say the least. When Finn went on a killing spree with the bad guys, he wasn't normally thinking of the cleanup afterward, and that night wasn't an exception.

More than a few of the thralls had been cut clean in half, spilling their blood and guts in wide arcs of bright red and purple viscera.

It looked like Salvador Dali and Jackson Pollock had teamed up and foregone paints in favor of the remains of soulless human husks controlled by an evil space alien that drove his victims insane by invading their dreams and being an all-around asshole.

Mila nodded to herself. Yeah, it looked exactly like that.

"I guess we should give Herman and Garret a call," Finn suggested and pulled out his phone.

"I don't think we want to get the Huldu involved. They're still pretty upset about the last time with the Dark Star." Mila smirked. She liked the two gnomes, so she didn't want to get them involved if she didn't have to. Besides, they had their hands full doing their part to keep *Earth* running smoothly. Well, as smoothly as they could, considering it was a few thousand years overdue for an oil change.

"You have a better idea?"

Mila smiled at the fact that there wasn't even a lick of sarcasm in his question. He genuinely thought she had a better idea. It was one of the reasons she loved him so much.

"I might." She walked over to the closest dead thrall and squatted for a closer look. She chose to squat instead of kneel so she wouldn't get blood on her pants—not that the enchanted leather would let the stain stay on their beautiful surface for long. She reached out and let her hand hover a few inches over the dead man's chest and tried to feel the body's aura.

For whatever reason, Mila had trouble seeing magic. She could feel it, and she could sense it, but she couldn't get her mind's eye to see it. The overtly obvious stuff was easy to see—even an unawakened Peabrain could see overt magic—but when it came to the subtle things like auras or the glow of magical tattoos, she was mostly blind. She caught things every once in a while, like the crown of tattoos around Finn's head that marked him as royalty, but it was fleeting at best and usually only from the periphery of her vision, and never when she was trying.

But, she'd been practicing with Finn and Victoria to feel the subtle magics that permeated most things, and had become passingly adequate at it.

Mila closed her eyes and reached out with what she thought of as her magic tentacle. It was a creepy image, but reasonably accurate. She formed some of her power into a long thin strand and ran it over whatever she wanted to "see" the magic in. As the faint magic reacted with hers, she started to draw a picture of what it should look like. The process reminded Mila of reading Braille. Luckily, she didn't need to get a clear picture of what little aura the husk of a man before her retained. She only wanted to confirm that the infernal magic was still in the dead body, and when her tentacle recoiled at the opposing magic, it confirmed her suspicion.

"Do you remember when I told you about Heather's death?" Mila rose and stood next to Finn.

"Yeah. What about it?"

"Remember how I said she turned to dust when Azoth had pulled all the power out of her like there was nothing left to hold it together?" Finn nodded, and Mila crossed her arms while looking down at the body. "Well, I think the same thing can happen here. He already stripped out the soul and the power that came with it, but before the body could collapse he replaced that power with a little of his. If I can strip the infernal power out of the body, it should crumble to dust."

"You think you can do that?" Finn's brows rose.

Mila nodded. "Yeah, I think I can. Why don't you use a

little of that earth magic to fix the holes you put in the road, and I'll see what I can do with the bodies."

"If you can do it to the dead, do you think you could do it to the living?"

Mila considered that. "Maybe, but I feel like there would be some sort of safety involved with an active thrall. Otherwise, the Valkyrie would have figured it out a long time ago. I'm betting that it has something to do with the active connection to Azoth."

Finn clucked his tongue. "Shame. That would have made things a lot easier. I'll get started on the road, but we should hurry. I knocked Missy pretty hard, but she's one tough bitch. She won't stay out forever."

Mila nodded and squatted again to get to work.

In the end, the process was a lot easier than Mila had suspected. All she had to do was take that magical tentacle and jam it into the body. Her celestial and Azoth's infernal magics sparked and fizzed, and after a second or two, they canceled each other out. As soon as she withdrew her magic, the body instantly crumbled to fine dust that the light breeze picked up to swirl away into the night.

By the time Finn completed the road repairs and had Missy's limp body over his shoulder, Mila was finishing with the last body.

"That was quick," Finn observed, trying in vain to pull Missy's pleated miniskirt down over her exposed panties. "Stupid thing can't be six inches long. Who wears stuff like this?" he grumbled, finally giving up and flopping her skinny limp form into his arms and carrying her like a child.

Mila laughed. "Why do you care if her ass is hanging out? She obviously doesn't."

"Because when she put on this glorified belt this morning, I'm sure she expected to be walking around on her two feet where the skirt hides the important bits, not bent over my shoulder as I carried her down the street. If she had, she probably would've worn pants. Nobody likes their ass on display for the entire world to see. Because she's insane doesn't mean she's not a person."

Mila leaned over and kissed his arm as they walked toward the condo, giving him an exaggerated sad puppy dog face.

"What?" Suspicion was thick in his voice.

"You are the sweetest man I know. You're also the most naïve if you think there aren't people that want other people looking at their butts all day. Have you heard of the Internet? You can find anything on there, even people who like to show off their butts. A *lot* of people who like to show off their butts."

"I'm well aware." Finn's face went a shade of red. "I once used the computer after Remmy had been goofing around on it. Let's just say she didn't close out her tabs, and that she is *not* shy about what she likes."

Mila laughed. "You're telling me you don't think Missy's skirt is sexy?"

He cleared his throat. "I didn't say that."

"Really?" Mila bit her lip then giggled quietly. "You know, I had a pretty good conversation with Remmy in San Francisco. She made me realize that I gave up something I liked for no good reason."

"What does that have to do with Missy's skirt?" Finn

turned sideways and went through the front door into the lobby as Mila held it open for him.

"I like her style. Maybe I'll order a skirt like that. You know, since you said it was sexy and all."

He grinned down at her. "You would wear something this short out in public?"

"Well, maybe it would be for around the house." She pressed the button for the elevator.

After a few seconds of silence as they waited for the doors to open, Finn cleared his throat, obviously having run a few scenarios through his head. "I could get into a micro-skirt on you."

"Yeah, you could." She drew out the "yeah" and nodded like a frat boy.

"You are so weird."

"Yeah, I am," she replied in the same suggestive manner.

CHAPTER ELEVEN

Mila followed Finn through the front door, the unconscious Missy still in his arms. Victoria and Remmy were waiting, obviously having watched the battle from the balcony.

Finn made a beeline for the couch where he put Missy before returning to the kitchen and rummaging through the junk drawer, looking for something to restrain her with before she woke up.

Victoria stood over Missy, her face a mix of anger and confusion. Mila felt like she knew what the woman was going through, if only from the outside. Remmy stood beside the tall blonde Valkyrie, her hand rubbing comforting circles on the small of Victoria's back as she kept her keen goblin eyes on the unconscious woman.

"Did Penny ever finish those anti-magic shackles? I know she was fairly close after studying the ones you brought back from San Francisco." Finn pulled out a roll of duct tape as he spoke and considered it for a few seconds before deciding it would do.

"I'm not sure." Mila headed toward the dojo and Penny's room on the other side of the open area. "I'll check. Victoria, can you keep her contained if she wakes up?"

"I can, but it might get a little violent. You okay with some broken furniture?" she said with a tight-lipped frown.

"I'm fine with it as long as no one gets seriously hurt."

"You know that's not going to do anything, right?" Victoria said to Finn as he leaned down to wrap Missy's wrists in the silver tape. "She might look small and dainty, but she's still a Valkyrie. Even if we lock away her powers, she would be strong enough to rip that whole roll in half."

Finn hesitated and looked up at Victoria. "What would you suggest?"

She held up her hand, and a ball of glowing celestial magic formed in it. "I suggest we use overwhelming force."

Mila missed the rest of the conversation as she turned to Penny's small door situated halfway up the wall beside the full-sized door into the dragon's room and knocked three times.

There was no reaction after a few seconds, which was odd. Penny was always active to some degree. Even when she was sleeping, she could be awake and alert in moments. When thirty seconds passed with no sign of Penny coming to the door, Mila tried again, this time knocking harder and longer before leaning in to hear any sounds coming from the room.

There was a distinct rustling sound followed by something with a lot of small parts falling over. Ten seconds later the little door opened a crack, and Penny stuck a sleepy face out into the light. She kept her eyes hooded and licked her lips a few times while she slowly focused.

"You okay?" Mila asked, real concern in her voice. She'd never seen Penny this out of it before.

After a few seconds, Penny nodded. "Chi shir. Shee?"

A little under the weather? That alone was surprising. She had never known the dragon to be sick in the least. Mila was about to press her further, but the sound of Finn and Victoria arguing about how best to keep Missy under control pressed her to answer Penny's question about what she needed.

"Did you ever finish the anti-magic shackles? We captured Missy. She's out for now, but she'll be waking up any second and we don't want her to have access to her magic for obvious reasons."

Penny's eye ridges rose slightly and she craned her neck around the small doorjamb, watching Finn and Victoria for a second before nodding. "Chi chi. Shir shee."

Penny's head pulled back through the gap in the door, and Mila saw her slowly head down the shelf she'd been standing on as she went to get the magic-canceling bracelets she'd finished but hadn't yet turned into shackles. Mila could only get the occasional glimpse and she didn't want to pry too much, but what she did see was an unusually slow-moving Penny who was waddling more than walking. Mila figured she must have some joint pain since that was a fairly common symptom for Mila when she had the flu.

A few seconds later, two golden bracelets were passed out of the crack followed by Penny's head. "Squee shir."

Mila turned the bracelets over in her hand, inspecting

them while she absorbed the information that only a registered person could remove them, and Penny's directive to
be sure that a few people could work them. They were
rather plain-looking cut circlets of flexible metal, so to put
them on you had to bend the metal and expand the
opening to slip them over the wearer's wrists. It didn't look
all that secure to Mila. She was about to question the
design, but Penny's slowly drooping head made her change
her mind. Penny wouldn't give her something without
knowing if it would work or not. She would trust the little
dragon's word on this one.

"Do you need anything? I could bring you a snack or
something. Feeding a cold always works for me."

Penny's head bobbed up as if she had been falling asleep
at the door. She smiled tiredly. "Chi chi."

Mila nodded and touched her cheek gently. "Okay, if
you're sure you're all set. Go back to bed. If you need
anything, call."

With a nod, Penny withdrew her head and closed the
door with a click.

Mila frowned, but she didn't want to press her friend if
it was only a cold or something. Penny would be back to
normal in no time.

Heading back into the living room, Mila ignored the
pointless argument over whether Finn could rip himself
out of duct tape-wrapped hands, and leaned over the back
of the couch and slipped the bracelets over Missy's wrists.

The argument died away when they saw what she was
doing.

The golden hoops became fluid once they were in
contact with Missy for a few seconds and flowed around

her small wrists, forming a skin-tight continuous ring of golden metal. After another few seconds, the liquid quality of the metal faded and the bracelets became solid once again.

They all watched for some sign that they'd worked, but there didn't seem to be any difference in the unmoving Valkyrie.

"Did they work?" Victoria asked.

Mila shrugged. "I don't know, but the fact that Penny said they would is good enough for me."

"Me. too." Finn pulled a finger-long piece of purple chalk from his harness and headed for the front door.

They all watched as he wrote an incredibly complicated rune set on the metal door. The design made Mila's eyes hurt to look at it. He leaned back and studied the whole thing for a second before nodding and pressing his palm to the center of the design. The crackle of magic filled the air as purple energy flowed from his arm and into the rune set. The power built and concentrated into the chalk lines until they glowed brighter than the lights in the hall. There was a flash of power that left green spots in Mila's vision and Finn stepped back, the rune set pulsing slightly on the door.

"That will keep her in the main area of the condo. She won't be able to leave or go anywhere but the kitchen, living room, and bathroom. Not sure about the dojo— there really isn't a rune for that, so I had to make something up. Either way, she won't be able to leave." He stretched his neck and rolled his shoulders, then slipped the chalk back into the little pocket on his harness. "Quite the morning. Kicked some ass and took a captive? That sounds like a cause for celebration. Who wants pancakes?"

"Not Penny, evidently." Mila's brows rose slightly as she looked at Finn.

The dwarf frowned and glanced at the small door to Penny's room. "Is she okay?"

Mila shrugged. "She said she wasn't feeling well. When I asked if she wanted a snack, she said she was too tired. I don't think I've ever heard her refuse a snack. Has she ever slept this much?"

Finn frowned at the door for a good long while as if trying to see through it with his mind. Eventually, his face softened, and Mila swore the corner of his mouth rose slightly in a hint of a grin. "If she's not feeling well, then it's best to let her deal with it on her own. She's a smart one and knows her limits. If she needs help, she'll ask for it."

"Well, Penny might not want pancakes, but I do." Remmy slapped her taut belly through the t-shirt she was still wearing as a dress and headed for the kitchen.

Mila looked back toward Penny's room for a few seconds, pushing her worry to the side. Finn was right. If Penny needed something, she would let them know.

"You want bacon in your pancakes?" Finn called from the kitchen, pulling Mila back to the issue at hand.

"Bacon in pancakes? Are you people animals?" Victoria asked with disgust.

Finn popped up from behind the counter, a mixing bowl in his hands. He stared at Victoria in shock. "Oh, man. You're in for a real treat."

Mila went to the coffeemaker and started making a pot

while laughing at the look on Victoria's face. "Don't worry. It's delicious."

"Do you have any Cheetos you could put in mine?" Remmy settled onto one of the high stools at the kitchen island.

This time, it was Mila's turn to look disgusted. "Okay, that's nasty."

CHAPTER TWELVE

Two hours later, they'd eaten and taken showers in shifts while they waited for Missy to wake up. Mila was worried that Finn had done real damage to the woman and maybe she wouldn't wake up ever again.

When she brought up her concern, Victoria laughed it off. She was tucked into the corner of the couch reading a novel while Remmy leaned against her and played a game on her phone.

"Valkyries are surprisingly hardy. You might be the only one I've seen who can force a self-heal, but we all heal eventually. She'll wake up. Soon, if my guess is right." Victoria peered at Missy over the spine of her novel. "Speak of the devil."

Missy moaned as she reached up to rub the side of her face. The spot where Fragar had smashed into her was swollen and red, but not nearly as bad as it should have been.

Mila and Finn came in from the kitchen. Mila sat on the coffee table in front of the still-groggy Valkyrie, and

Finn stood behind Missy, towering over the back of the couch.

After half a minute of rubbing her face and moaning, Missy's eyes snapped open and she spun to a sitting position, her face wide with shock as she locked gazes with Mila.

"Morning, sleepyhead." Mila smiled as she sipped her coffee.

Anger instantly replaced the shock as Missy raised a hand and pointed the palm at Mila's chest. They sat like that for a beat before Missy jabbed her hand at Mila again, then looked at it like it was a jammed gun.

"What the fuck have you done to me?" she shouted, noticing the bracelets and trying to pull them off to no avail.

"You wanted to know where my building was. Well, here you are." Mila calmly waved a hand around the room like it was a showcase on a game show.

Missy looked around and seemed to notice the others for the first time. She slowly backed into the couch, pulling her knees up to provide some semblance of protection. That was until she noticed Finn behind her and flinched down into the cushions.

Mila snapped her fingers, getting the fallen Valkyrie's attention. "Hey, over here. You and I are going to have a conversation. This has all gone on long enough, and we need to end it. Tell me where Azoth is hiding and what his plans are, and I promise you I'll do whatever I can to free you from his influence. You can get out of this, but you need to help us out. I promise I'll do my best to protect you."

Missy stared at Mila, blinking slowly from behind her knees wrapped in her thin arms. It looked like Missy was considering the offer, even going as far as nodding slightly, but when she opened her mouth to speak no sound emerged. She strained, but couldn't force the words out. She tried one more time, tears in her eyes, then her jaw snapped shut and a distant madness slowly filled her blue eyes.

Mila frowned and leaned forward, elbows on her knees. "I want to help you. You made some stupid decisions, and you'll have to pay for them one way or another, but no one deserves to be that creature's slave. Give me something. Anything."

Missy suddenly burst into gales of laughter, her knees falling to the sides so she was sitting cross-legged on the couch. She threw her head back, laughter still belting out of her and tears running down her cheeks.

Mila drew a deep breath, leaned back, and frowned. She didn't find any of this funny, and it was getting them nowhere. "Don't you *want* to be free of him?"

The laughter cut off and Missy's head dropped to face Mila with a crazed look. "Don't you get it, little child? I can't be free. He has hold of me in a way that you can't pry loose. I'm his creature now and nothing but death will free me, but I can't kill myself to be free. I've tried, and he stopped me with a thought. How do you, the smallest and weakest of us all, think you could compete with his power? He will eat you for a snack before you can say two words."

Mila smiled. Finally, something she could work with. "We have a plan. And I never said I would fight him alone."

Missy snorted with derision. "What, these losers? You

like watching your friends turned into monsters intent on ripping your throat out? How about it, big guy?" she asked Finn, tilting her head back so she could look up at him. "You want to rip your girlfriend's pretty little throat out? Yeah...I didn't think so."

"Azoth won't turn anyone against me," Mila responded with more confidence than she felt. "We have a way to destroy his body. This is a plan that started back in the first battle with him. It will work."

"Destroy his body?" she cackled with laughter at the idea. "He's a Drude. He'll grow it back. You would have to destroy the body to nothing but pure energy. If even one speck remains he'll return, and we'll be in the same position we always are. You could drop him into the heart of *Earth*'s great engines and he would still walk back out eventually."

"That only happens if he has infernal magic stored away to power the regrowth. We plan on taking care of that," Mila explained, not wanting to get too far into the details just in case.

"He's fully awake now, with his powers replenished. Every day, he grows beyond what we fought all those years ago, and that took twenty Valkyries working together to put him to sleep. You don't stand a chance. You cannot win. My only option is to trust that he will keep his word and take me away from this forsaken excuse for a ship."

Missy folded her arms across her chest and slumped into the couch, obviously understanding that she had no power to try to escape, but was also not going to help anymore. Mila saw that the fear and madness had taken greater hold of the woman than she had initially thought. They were done for now.

Mila stood and moved around the couch, nodding for Finn to follow, and walked to the kitchen. On their way past Danica's room, the door opened and the tall elf came out, scratching her side under the tank top she'd slept in.

"Hey, guys." She yawned and turned to wave at Victoria and Remmy, then froze when she saw Missy sitting on the couch. "What the hell?"

"Don't worry." Mila patted her arm. "Her magic is locked away, and no one knows we have her yet. She can't escape, and she can't hurt us."

Danica blinked a few times, then nodded. "Okay. That's one way to wake up. Shit, I need some coffee."

Mila let Danica pass them and stepped close to Finn. "I think we need to go talk to this mystery woman. She might have something we can use, and with Missy out of the fight, we might have a chance of catching Azoth with his pants down."

Finn nodded in agreement. "If anyone would know where Azoth is, it would be Yaminah. I agree we need to talk to her. She might be the only person on the planet who wants Azoth dead more than you."

Mila rolled her eyes. "We don't know that it's Yaminah. For all we know, she's dead. I fucked her up pretty badly in that last fight."

"Either way, we need a good place to meet her. Somewhere out of the way, where if things go bad we can kick her ass without having to worry about collateral damage." Finn tugged his beard as he wracked his brain.

"Great Sand Dunes National Park," Danica said from

the kitchen before adding a little cream to her coffee. When Mila and Finn both looked at her, she reddened a little. "Sorry, but I can't help overhearing you. I'm an elf, remember? You wouldn't believe the things I overhear."

Mila waved Danica over to join the quiet conversation. She licked the coffee off her teaspoon and put it in the sink before coming around the island and standing close.

"I've never been to the dunes. Where are they?" Mila glanced over her shoulder to be sure Missy wasn't listening.

"About three hours south of here." Danica loudly sipped her coffee before continuing. "They're huge. A lot of people go to the park, but they mostly stay on the edges and around the tall dune. That still leaves about fifty square miles of empty dunes. You could probably blow up a car out in the middle of the park and no one would notice."

"Can you take us there? I don't want to spend six hours in the car if we don't have to."

Danica nodded and flipped her hair over her shoulder before sipping again. "When do you want to go?"

Finn and Mila exchanged glances, and he shrugged and nodded.

"How about right now?" Mila asked.

Danica looked out the window at the now-rising sun. "Okay, but can I put on something more than a tank top and shorts?"

Mila snorted. "Sure. We'll be out here when you're ready."

After walking back into the living room, Mila reached over the back of the couch and patted Remmy on the shoulder. The little goblin looked up from her game and smiled. "What's up? You need me to stab someone?"

"Why would..." Mila started, but then shrugged. "Maybe. You down for watching my back with Finn?"

Remmy looked at Victoria, who was pretending to read but had been staring at Missy, waiting for her to make a move. She frowned, then shrugged and hopped up onto the cushion and vaulted over the back of the couch to land beside Mila.

"Yeah, I'm down for a little back watching. The boss man and I will keep you clear. Besides, it looks like the fun here is a little distracted. I'll grab my leathers and weapons. Be back in a sec." She sprinted for the door.

Mila watched her go, then glanced down at Victoria and once again decided she needed to ask Remmy what was up there.

"Victoria, we're going to step out for a meeting. Keep an eye on our guest, and for the love of God don't stab her while we're gone. She could still be useful."

Jumping a little as if she'd been caught watching porn, Victoria turned and nodded at Mila. "Don't worry about us. Just two old friends spending the morning on the couch. Not talking. And not stabbing one another."

"Okay." Mila drew it out uncomfortably. "We shouldn't be more than an hour."

"No problem. Take your time."

Victoria turned back to stare at Missy, who was picking black nail polish off her fingernails and looking like a goth teen that had been yelled at by her overbearing parents. If Mila didn't know any better, she would have felt sorry for the elder Valkyrie.

CHAPTER THIRTEEN

Mila stood leaning back against Finn's chest while holding Remmy close to hers, keeping the group's size small enough that Danica could teleport them all at the same time. The large bubble formed around them and Mila waved to Victoria who stood with her arms crossed watching them go. The Valkyrie was raising her hand to wave back when the bubble popped.

One second, Mila was looking at the inside of her condo. The next, the early morning sun nearly blinded her as it reflected off the mountains of white sand that suddenly appeared all around them.

Closing her eyes and wincing in pain, Mila blindly reached into her pocket and pulled out the sunglasses she had brought for this situation.

Remmy and Finn stepped away to give themselves some room as they all found the sunglasses they had brought. By the time Mila had her glasses on, she was blinking the burn spots from her vision.

"You can call me when you need a ride back." Danica stepped away from them to form a return bubble.

"Thanks. Hey, when you get back, be sure to keep an eye on Victoria." Mila bit her lip for a second before continuing. "It's not that I don't trust her, but she's pretty emotional about this whole thing. And remember, if shit goes down, grab the Reaper and get to Rebecca's place right away. Keeping that weapon out of Azoth's greasy hands is the number one priority."

Danica nodded. "Got it." She frowned. "Where did you hide it? I noticed it wasn't on the TV stand like it was when I went to bed."

Mila chuckled and looked over at Finn, who had suggested the new hiding place. "Sorry, I forgot we moved it after bringing Missy in. Didn't want to tempt her to try anything stupid. We hid it under the kitchen sink, behind the trash bin."

"Under the sink? Why would you hide it there?"

Finn answered, obviously feeling like he needed to defend his choice. "Would you look under the kitchen sink if you were looking for a weapon powerful enough to end an entire world?"

Danica tilted her head and pursed her lips. "I guess not. That's a pretty good hiding place."

"See? I told you it was a good idea," Finn smiled down at Mila.

She laughed. "I didn't say it wasn't, babe," she consoled, patting his arm before turning back to Danica. "Keep your distance from Missy. Even if her powers are locked up, it doesn't mean she's not extremely dangerous. She has thousands of years of combat experience. Be sure you always have a way out of the condo."

"What about Penny? Last night, she said she wasn't feeling well. Is she still in her room?"

Finn waved away the concern. "She'll be fine. She put down a set of protection runes in her room in preparation for her eggs. She's going to be one of those helicopter parents for sure."

Mila gave him a sideways look. "Where did you learn the term helicopter parent?"

"Remmy watches one of those reality shows about teen parents. It was…eye-opening," he added with a deep frown.

"That show is awesome." Remmy pulled the hood of her leather bodysuit over her head. Her white braid hung out of it and down to her waist. "It reminds me that there are some Peabrains out there as fucked up as us goblins. Makes me feel like a real member of society."

"Huh. That might be the most legitimate reason I've ever heard to watch that show." Mila chuckled.

"Okay, I'm out of here. Be careful, and I'll see you in a while." Danica stepped forward to give Mila a quick hug before forming another large bubble and disappearing with a soft popping noise.

Mila slowly turned in a circle, taking in their surroundings. They stood at the bottom of a valley between two huge dunes that had to be a hundred feet tall at their peaks. At the ends of the valley were more dunes from the staggered formation of the wind-blown sand piles. The effect was that they were essentially at the bottom of a bowl of white sand.

Mila tested the ground to check for movement and

found the sand under her feet was relatively solid, even if it seemed to be shifting fairly easily the further up the slope she looked.

"I'm surprised we're not sinking," Remmy commented, hopping from one foot to the other, obviously not having spent much time in the sand.

"It's all about time and pressure," Mila explained. "Down here, the sand is fairly protected from the wind so it has time to settle and firm up. Plus, when it rains this ground becomes saturated, which compacts it even further. Over enough time, it will compact down to sandstone. On the slopes you'll probably sink a few inches, maybe a foot, so be careful."

"How do you know all that?" Remmy looked up the closest slope.

"They don't call me Dr. Winters for nothing." Mila grinned. "Okay, how do we do this? Hit the call button and see what happens?"

"I think we should hide and see what she does when she shows up," Remmy suggested.

Mila considered, but eventually shook her head. "There's nowhere for us all to hide. We would have to get over the tops of the dunes before she showed up."

"Perhaps we do a little of both ideas?" Finn suggested and continued when Mila gave him a questioning look. "We have two people hide and the third waits out in the open. That way, the one out in the open keeps her attention and gives the other two a better chance of staying hidden. I'll wait here with the stone and you two head to the dunes' tops. You can cover me if things go south."

"Good idea, but I'll be the one down here." Mila held up

a hand to stop Finn's complaint. "I know you don't want me to get hurt, but you're going to have to accept that I'm a capable woman who can take care of herself...mostly. Besides, she wants to talk to me, not you. If she shows up and you're standing here, she might leave."

Finn looked like he wanted to argue, but he nodded instead. "That might be better. I can hide right here, and Remmy can hold her breath to become invisible."

"You can hide right here?" Mila looked around them at the flat ground. "Where?"

"Darlin', I'm a dwarf. Sand to a dwarf might as well be thick air for all it slows us down. Remmy, wait until you see some kind of teleport, then hold your breath. You'll need time to move into their blind spot before you need to take another breath." Remmy nodded and moved twenty feet or so away so she could watch the whole area. "Ready?"

Mila shrugged exaggeratedly. "I guess so. I'm waiting on Finn to find this miraculous hiding place."

He chuckled and knelt to place his palm on the ground, flexing his fingers slightly so that they dug into the sand. "Want to see a magic trick?"

Mila laughed. "Sure."

Finn's hand glowed bright purple for a second. Then he dropped into the sand as if it had turned into water. Mila jumped back, her hand going to her mouth as she stifled a yelp of surprise.

"Holy fuck!" Remmy shouted, her eyes wide enough that Mila could see the whites all around them even from a distance.

"I told you it was easy." Finn's muffled voice filtered

through the slightly swirled sand he'd fallen through.

Mila jumped again at the sound of his voice. "Are you okay down there?"

"I mean, it's not comfortable, but I'll manage. Let's get this party started," he shouted, his muffled voice making him sound monotone.

"Okay, I'm pressing the stone."

Mila pulled the blue button-shaped stone from her jacket pocket and nodded to Remmy. The goblin nodded back while pulling her daggers and dropping into a ready position, her eyes scanning the area for the slightest change.

Mila swallowed and squeezed the stone between her thumb and forefinger.

Nothing seemed to happen. There was no flash of light or beeping sound. The stone didn't glow or grow warm in her fingers. It felt like a regular stone.

Mila squeezed it again, and still nothing.

Shaking the stone in her hand to theoretically knock something loose, Mila looked up at Remmy. "Are you sure—"

Remmy sucked in a breath and vanished.

Mila frowned, then realized what that meant and turned to see a void portal opening up. "Oh, fuck," she murmured to herself as she pulled Gram out, whispering its power word as she did so.

A robed figure stepped out of the portal, making Mila nearly jump in and cut it down, thinking that Azoth was coming through. But the form was far too small to be the Drude and obviously female.

The figure had her hands up, showing that her palms

were both empty and not glowing with magic. A deep and unnaturally dark hood covered the woman's head, hiding any clue about who she was. Mila saw that the hands and forearms, which had been exposed when the robe's sleeves fell to the figure's elbows, were covered in long black leather gloves that hid her skin.

"Peace," the woman said in a raspy, dry voice. "I'm here to offer my help."

Mila pointed Gram at the woman's chest, which was only a lunge away. "Who are you, and why should I trust you?"

The void portal snapped shut, cutting off any quick escape for the woman, and making Mila feel a little better knowing that enemies weren't about to pour out of it and overrun her. She tensed once again, however, when the woman reached up to her hood and grasped the edges of the cowl.

"Don't you recognize your handiwork, Valkyrie?" she rasped as she threw the hood back.

Mila's eyes went wide.

The woman's skin was shiny and pink with new skin in long swirling patterns while a darker, almost charred color filled in the rest. Thin lines formed ridges where the two colors met, as if someone welded them together. At first, Mila thought the woman was some sort of Frankenstein's monster, but the dense fern-like pattern was too regular. Closer inspection revealed that the markings were burns where the new skin was still raw while the old skin looked overcooked.

She was completely hairless—even her eyelashes were

missing—and when she tried to smirk, the corner of her mouth pulled at a slightly off angle.

Despite all the differences, the intense green eyes were the same.

"Yaminah." Mila lowered the sword slightly.

A muffled and barely audible, "Told ya!" filtered up from the sand beside her.

Mila wanted to say something to the smug bastard, but it was evident that Yaminah hadn't heard Finn. That jerk knew how loud he could be and still stay undetected.

The burned and scarred woman tilted her head, her green eyes locked on Mila. "Shall we make a deal, or fight to the death? At this point, either would be fine with me. Welcome, even."

Mila saw none of the madness in Yaminah's green eyes that she had witnessed in Missy's, or even the last time she had seen Yaminah herself. Her eyes showed physical pain in the tightness at the corners, but they also had a spark in them that spoke of a quick and efficient mind.

Mila lowered Gram to her side. "Let's talk first. Depending on what you say, maybe a fight after."

"That's my girl." Finn rumbled with pride.

CHAPTER FOURTEEN

Yaminah slowly reached into her robe, keeping her left hand up to show that she wasn't trying anything stupid. Mila tensed but let the woman continue, wanting to see where this was going.

Pulling her hand out of the brown robes, Yaminah held a crystal-clear cube two inches to a side between her thumb and finger. She held the cube out to Mila but didn't move to get closer.

"What is it?" Mila showed no indication that she intended to touch the thing.

"It's a spell I've been working on for when I could secure outside help. This cube is tied to Azoth's robes. It uses them as a focal point. With it, you'll be able to view Azoth and his surroundings without him knowing. I'm not sure how helpful it will be now that he's set a deadline for you, but it can't hurt, and it shows that I'm willing to betray him." She focused on the cube, her eyes narrowing slightly.

Blue and green magic swirled at the cube's center before quickly spiraling out to surround her and Mila.

Gram came up as Mila stepped forward. She pressed the sword's razor-sharp tip to the hollow of Yaminah's neck. The other woman didn't flinch, as if she knew it would happen but hadn't had a choice.

Hesitating at the lack of reaction, combined with the worried look on Yaminah's face, Mila glanced around and saw that the interior of the green and blue swirls showed a slightly transparent 360-degree view centered above Azoth. Mila looked down and saw the top of Azoth's hood below her.

The Drude sat on a throne made of solid stone, unmoving with his back straight as a board and hands resting on the thick armrests. She watched for a few seconds, but he didn't move. He was so still that Mila thought it might be a still image or a trick. She was about to demand that Yaminah explain when she saw Azoth's long gray finger tap on the stone.

"He can't sense us?" Mila slowly pulled Gram back, a bead of bright red blood rolling down Yaminah's collarbone where the tip of the sword had punctured a tiny hole in her ruined skin.

Yaminah swallowed and shook her head. "His body is infused with infernal magic to the point that it makes it impossible to even try and read his aura without him noticing, but his robes are mundane cloth. By casting the anchor to the robe, he can't feel it in the slightest. Technically, we're spying on his robes, not him."

Mila raised an eyebrow at the enthusiasm she heard in Yaminah's voice for the spellwork. It was a clear change from the zealot she'd originally met in the Market all those weeks ago. If anything, that was what convinced Mila most that Yaminah had broken free of the curse.

"Clever." Mila leaned back and dropped Gram's tip to her side. "But turn it off. I have questions for you, and I don't want this to distract us." In reality, she didn't want Remmy or Finn to have a blocked view of the two of them and decide to attack.

The image vanished as the green and blue energy faded to mist and quickly dissipated into the air. Yaminah tossed the cube down at Mila's feet and stepped back, giving them room to talk.

"Keep the cube. It'll be useful even if you don't want my help."

Mila glanced down at the thing sticking half out of the sand and wondered if it would be a mistake to take it back to the condo. What guarantee was there that it didn't have a tracking spell embedded in it? Mila felt the stone button she still held in her free hand. If Yaminah wanted to track her then she would have enchanted the stone, but the wards Penny put up would have broken any such spell and warned them that someone had tried to sneak it into the building. Nothing like that had happened.

If shit were going to go down, it would be best if it happened out in the dunes. That's why they'd come out here in the first place. Mila made up her mind, reached down, and picked up the cube, half expecting to have her arm blown off by some booby trap, but nothing happened. It merely felt like a glass cube with a good heft to it.

Yaminah stood holding her hands in front of her like a shy child.

"How did you break the Geas? Shouldn't you be dead for giving me this?" Mila tucked both the stone and the cube into her jacket pocket.

The corner of Yaminah's mouth twitched up into a dark smile. "That fucking thing took me the longest to overcome. In the end, a Geas is a contest of wills, mine against his. I realized early on that I couldn't break the Geas while he focused on it, but the more he trusted me the less he did to maintain the curse. But the truth is that I owe you a debt of gratitude for doing this to me." She touched the motley skin at her throat.

Mila raised an eyebrow at that. "Thank me? I figured you would want to kill me for doing that."

A snorting laugh turned into a cough that ended when Yaminah spat on the sand, leaving speckles of blood. "Because you had reduced my body to barely more than a husk, Azoth wrote me off as weak and broken. He wouldn't allow me to take a healing potion as punishment for my failure with you. Instead, he's making me heal slowly and painfully. I'll be scarred for life if I let it go too long, and he knows that. He is cruel for cruelty's sake. But, he no longer thought of me as capable and turned his focus on breaking Missy completely. My body was broken, but my mind was still clear. The moment he turned his focus from me, I cast a counter-curse that snuffed out the Geas and freed me from its repercussions."

"If you're free, then why not leave?"

"I'm free of the Geas, not of Azoth himself. I still carry his taint inside me. He can still order me to do things, and I will have to do them, but only as long as he is directly controlling me. As soon as he shifts his focus, I am free once again." She smashed her fist into her hand. "We can use that to tip the balance. He will never see an attack coming from someone he has written off as weak. I'm a student of magic and have skills he knows nothing of. I can hurt him, but I can't destroy him. Together, though…"

"Won't he simply command you to stop?"

"Eventually, but it will take him a few seconds to comprehend what's happening. I don't know if you've noticed, but he's not particularly smart. Only powerful."

"And cruel." Mila glanced at Yaminah's skin. "What's your idea?"

"When you make your move, I'll hit him from behind. I'll be able to stun him, if only for a few moments, but it should be enough for you to cut him down."

Mila considered the woman. She was practically pleading to be used as a distraction so there was a slightly better chance of gaining her freedom. Mila couldn't say she would do anything different in Yaminah's shoes.

"You're putting a lot of trust in my ability to kill him before he comes after you."

Yaminah set her jaw and looked Mila up and down. "I am. But, I'm betting that you might be the only one capable of pulling it off."

"You realize you're betting your life on that." Mila frowned.

Yaminah nodded. "I do."

"What do you want in return?" Mila guessed that Azoth's death was only part of the plan.

She swallowed hard, then looked Mila in the eye. "When this is over, I want you to use the Reaper on me. I want you to take away the memories of what I've done. My time with Azoth, the people he made me kill—all of it. I want the chance to start over."

Mila could see how that would be worth the risk. She couldn't imagine having to commit atrocities against your will and remember every detail.

Mila nodded.

"Behind you!" Remmy shouted, making Yaminah spin around in surprise to find the goblin five feet behind her, her daggers out and teeth bared.

At the same time, Mila spun to see several void portals opening, and Rougarou starting to leap through.

Mila turned back to Yaminah, whose face had gone white as her jaw worked up and down, but no words came out. "What the hell is this?"

"I...I didn't call them. It wasn't me." Yaminah backed up and opened a void portal behind herself. "He must have thought I was trying to run and tracked me here. I'll return to him and say that I was trying to capture you, but you didn't have the Reaper on you. I'll think of something. Remember our deal. I'm counting on you." Then she stepped through the portal and was gone.

CHAPTER FIFTEEN

Penny felt like her insides were going to implode. At the same time, she felt relief that the two eggs she'd already laid during the night were out and safely cradled in the nest she'd created atop her hoard pile. It had been a harrowing and completely mind-boggling experience that she'd already decided she never wanted to go through again.

Unfortunately, the third and final egg was coming out right now, whether she wanted it or not.

She had thought that when the time came to lay her brood she would want someone with her, but when they had returned from Rebecca's and Lance's, Penny wanted nothing to do with anyone. It was an odd sensation, but one that she wasn't entirely unprepared for. Her mother had told her it would be that way, but like most children, Penny hadn't believed her. She should write a letter to her mother saying she was sorry.

That morning when Mila had come to the door asking for the bracelets, it was all Penny could do to answer. Not because she didn't have the strength, but because she didn't want to interact with people.

That interaction, while biologically unwelcome in her current state, had let Penny know Mila and Finn had some sort of captive in the condo. That alone wouldn't bother Penny since she'd warded her room all to hell, and Finn could take care of anything before it became a problem for her anyway. But the fact that five minutes ago, Penny had felt a surge of magic that told her Danica had teleported herself and at least three other people out of the condo, coupled with the sound of a struggle currently happening in the living room, was making Penny a little nervous.

She would have gone out to help whoever was fighting off the unknown prisoner, but her third egg had breached, and she needed to push it out before it tore her in half.

After closing her eyes, Penny used a mix of physical muscles to push while simultaneously using a large dose of magic to be sure the egg grew five times the size it started at before coming out. It was a delicate balance, and the loud banging and cursing in the other room weren't helping.

Not having a choice, Penny blocked out the sounds around her and began the process that once started couldn't be interrupted, or the egg might break or fail to grow completely.

Magic flowed from Penny's core through her abdomen, and the small egg greedily absorbed it. As she pushed, she felt an uncomfortable pressure that she was unfortunately becoming familiar with as the egg rapidly grew. She pushed more, moving the growing object farther along while it continued to enlarge.

Penny vaguely registered that the sounds of the struggle in the living room had ceased, but right now, that meant nothing to her.

She reached the halfway point, sweat and tears making her face glisten in the low light of the desk lamp she had turned on when Mila came to her door. Stopping the magic and the pushing, Penny drew a few breaths to recover before gritting her teeth and pushing once again. Her magic was flowing quickly now, and she needed to move fast. This was the critical moment.

Her flow increased, the egg grew, and she pushed. Flames puffed from her nostrils, making images dance through her closed eyelids.

The clicking sound of a door handle barely intruded into her consciousness.

She grunted while pushing for all she was worth, her magic flowing nearly out of control and making the egg grow rapidly as she reached the end.

"Oh, well, look at that. Maybe I'll have fried eggs before I go," a young female voice said, madness clear in its tone.

The sound startled Penny, making her cut her magic flow as her eyes snapped open. She immediately knew she'd made a mistake and started the flow again, adding more magic than her body was telling her to and trying to compensate for the momentary lapse, but it was too late.

The third and final egg fell into the nest of gold coins and gleaming gems with a solid metallic *thunk*.

Penny looked down at her third egg, her heart fluttering with worry when she saw that it was significantly smaller than the first two. That single-second lapse of magic had made an enormous difference.

After taking the egg in both hands, she felt the life inside stirring. Her chick would live, but its aura was much weaker than its siblings.

Penny gently nestled the egg into the coins beside the others and patted it lovingly, hoping it would grow to be strong despite its inauspicious birth. Only after she felt the eggs were safely in place and observed the power of the treasure hoard flowing properly, did she finally let herself come back to the issue at hand.

The serene face Penny had for her eggs fell away to be replaced with a stone-faced mask of murder.

As she turned to see who had dared to interrupt her birthing process and nearly killed one of her children, Penny felt smoldering flames roll out the sides of her mouth.

The utterly insane, smirking look on Missy's face fell away, replaced with the wide-eyed fear Penny had seen many times on prey right before she tore their throats out.

"Uh, kidding?" Missy's voice quivered.

Penny slowly stalked forward, her golden eyes locked with the Valkyrie's.

Missy held up a bloody chef's knife she had obviously taken from the kitchen. In her periphery, Penny saw Victoria lying on her back in the living room, a bright red bloodstain slowly spreading beneath her.

Missy shook the knife threateningly and stepped back from the open door. "Stay back, lizard! I will slice you up and eat you like sushi," she threatened with false bravado but took another step back as Penny continued stalking forward. "I'm sorry, I'll go. I didn't mean it. I need to get out of here. Please…"

Penny kept coming, her eyes beginning to glow with a fire all their own. She had promised herself that no one would threaten or hurt her children, and this insane zealot had done it before Penny even had the egg out of her body. She couldn't let that stand. It didn't matter how much Missy begged and pleaded—Penny had decided.

She was going to kill this bitch.

Pushing off the floor with everything her back legs could give, Penny launched herself at Missy's face.

The Valkyrie brought the knife up to slash at Penny's guts, but she saw it coming a mile away and reached out with her left hand and grabbed Missy's fingers wrapped around the knife's handle. Her talons sank into the flesh as she pulled herself forward, bringing her back feet up so they were the first thing that contacted the screaming Valkyrie's face.

Penny felt the skin of Missy's cheek and lips peel open as she raked her razor-sharp claws across them. Missy stumbled backward, throwing her head back to get away from the attack, but by then Penny had a handful of her short blue hair and was straddling the fallen Valkyrie's face.

Folding her free hand's talons into a single point, Penny jammed her fingers into Missy's left eye, driving through the eyelid and not stopping until she'd buried her entire hand in the bloody eye socket.

Missy's scream landed on deaf ears as Penny pulled her hand out, flinging blood and bits of eyeball into the air. She sucked in a breath and blew white-hot flame into the hole, cauterizing it instantly and filling the condo with the smell of cooking meat.

The knife clattered across the floor, and Missy reached up to grab Penny around the chest and rip her free. Using both hands, Missy threw her away.

Penny was faster than the magically dampened Valkyrie, though, and dug her front talons into the meat of Missy's forearms right below the elbow. The momentum of the throw caused Penny's claws to dig deep furrows down her arms and over her wrists.

Blood splattered to the ground in gouts as Penny's talons severed the arteries in both wrists. Unfortunately, that also meant her claws caught on the golden bracelets, and as their creator, they recognized her as one who could take them off the prisoner. The bands opened and slipped off Missy's gushing wrists, freeing her magic.

Penny hit the mats lining the floor of the dojo and rolled end-over-end, the golden hoops still in her hands.

A popping noise sounded, and Penny saw Danica appear in the living room then look around in surprise at the bloody melee. Spotting Missy trying to staunch the flow of blood from both wrists simultaneously, Danica immediately jumped into action. Penny watched as she vaulted over the couch and sprinted around the corner, heading for her room.

Penny didn't wait to see how it would all play out. She wanted to determine how it would play out. Penny launched herself at the stumbling Missy and shot a jet of white-hot flame at Missy's chest.

Missy dodged most of the flames by falling backward, but her blue hair burned away on the right side, leaving angry blisters that formed before she hit the floor.

To Penny's surprise, Missy flung out a hand and hit her

with a weak blast of black-tinged celestial magic, sending the little dragon soaring across the room to impact the far wall and fall to the floor.

Blood poured from Missy, and Penny knew she only had a few minutes to live, Valkyrie or not. Bleeding out killed anyone with a body, so it shocked Penny when Missy seemed to ignore her plight and shakily rose to her feet. The Valkyrie held out a limp hand, gathering as much power as she could in the sad-looking appendage, determined to blast Penny out of existence.

Penny flipped to her feet and charged, determined to dodge whatever the dying woman threw her way, but it turned out she didn't need to do any fancy footwork.

An arrow slammed into Missy's shoulder blade, making her spin to the left as she let the magic fly. The orb of power slammed into a rack of wooden practice swords, bursting the expertly carved replicas into splinters. A second arrow hit the thin woman in the kidney, punching all the way through and continuing across the room to lodge itself in the brick wall.

Missy must have finally realized how fucked she was because instead of fighting back, she created a void portal and fell through it, vanishing from the condo and Penny's wrath.

Danica sent four arrows through the portal before it closed, but they were literal shots in the dark. As soon as the portal snapped shut, Danica dropped her bow and the handful of arrows and ran to the small safe in the living room.

She punched in the code and quickly opened it, then pulled out a wooden box and threw open the lid. Nearly fifty vials of healing potion nestled in foam cutouts. It represented hundreds of thousands of dollars' worth of the precious fluid.

Danica pulled out a vial before she practically leaped the five feet to Victoria from her knees. She pulled the stopper and poured the red fluid into the unconscious woman's mouth, then began massaging her throat, trying to get her to swallow.

"Penny," Danica shouted while laying a hand on Victoria's chest, "are you hurt? Do you need a potion?"

Finn had found a woman through his friends at the Market who, unbelievably, had a recipe for a healing potion that would work on dragons. Finn had commissioned four of them to be made, in case. Each one cost more than the entire box of regular potions at Danica's feet.

Shaking with anger at what Missy had done, and hoping that those last four arrows finally finished the bitch off, Penny didn't answer. Instead, she turned and saw her hoard with the three eggs nestled into the shallow bowl she had formed atop the pile. The anger instantly moved to the back of her mind as she saw that while the last one was small, all three were perfect in every other way.

She had done it. Her family would live on for another generation, and her exile was over. She had brought honor to faerie dragon-kind and ensured they would persist for a while longer.

Penny suddenly slumped to the floor, her strength gone after the intense fight. She tried to crawl back to her eggs since they needed her to watch over them while they matured. She needed to be there when they broke free so they would imprint on her, and she could pass her intelligence on to them.

Otherwise, they would only be wild drakes, devoid of true intelligence.

Penny struggled, but she was too exhausted to do much more than flop her arm toward her hoard.

Gentle hands scooped her up off the floor.

Penny hissed and shot a warning flame up at whoever was trying to stop her from getting back to her eggs.

Danica screamed and dropped her before stumbling backward and falling on her ass. "What the fuck, Penny?" she shouted, checking to be sure she hadn't caught fire.

Penny felt bad about hissing. She hadn't meant to, but it came out. She couldn't help it.

The elf climbed to her feet and cautiously walked over to Penny and looked down at her as if she were trying to figure out whether she was the same dragon she had grown to love. Penny watched as Danica looked past her into the room with the hoard and the three eggs. Her face went from confused to wide-eyed excitement in a flash.

"Oh. My. God. Penny! Why didn't you say anything? You can hiss all you want, but I'm putting you with your babies." She leaned down to scoop Penny up but hesitated. "Don't catch my hair on fire, please."

Penny felt her hackles rise as Danica carefully picked her up again. A long low growl rumbled in her chest, making Danica quickly move into Penny's room and lay her in the shallow depression beside the eggs.

Penny felt thankful that Danica had helped, but there was an overwhelming evolutionary mechanism that was causing Penny to lash out at anything that wasn't her eggs right now. Penny watched with suspicious eyes as Danica backed out of the room and pulled the door to a crack, then stuck her head back in.

"Love you, Penny. You did great." Then she pulled the door closed, and the quiet hum of power flowing from the hoard into her three babies once again surrounded Penny.

The faerie dragon felt a pang of guilt and used a little of her magic stores to flick a finger at the wall. A message seared itself into the white paint, right where anyone entering the room would immediately see it. By the time the sizzling of boiled paint finally died, Penny was curled around her eggs and fast asleep.

CHAPTER SIXTEEN

Mila blasted a charging Rougarou into pieces of bloody pulp with a quick pull of the Ivar's trigger, then dropped to a knee as she ducked the slashing talons of a second wolfman and cut the legs out from under it. Finn chopped the thing's head off as soon as it hit the ground and gave her a wild-eyed grin before kicking another Rougarou in the crotch and sending it four feet into the air.

Blocking a set of talons meant for her face with Gram, Mila sent a shot of magical energy through her leg as she kicked the beast in the chest. There was a satisfying crunch, and blood sprayed from its mouth as it stumbled backward.

Remmy appeared beside the stumbling Rougarou and slashed its hamstring open before sucking in a breath and vanishing again. The creature stiffened a second later as a hole appeared in its chest, on its way to the sand.

They had killed a dozen of the monsters in the last five minutes, but the portals were still open, and Rougarou continued to pile through.

A popping noise behind Mila made her throw up a shield and point her gun at the source of the sound.

"What the fuck happened?" Danica shouted as she pulled an arrow from her hip quiver and sent it into the head of a Rougarou that had stepped through its portal. Her hands were blood-covered, but she didn't seem to be hurt.

"Danica, what are you doing here?" Mila shouted while sending a bolt from the Ivar and taking the head clean off a wolfman that had taken the elf's sudden appearance as a chance for a quick kill.

"Missy escaped. She stabbed Victoria and was attacking Penny when I got back. I forced a potion down Victoria's throat, but she was pretty bad off. She wanted me to come and warn you about a possible attack."

Mila focused on the one thing in that explanation that stood out most. "She attacked Penny? Is Penny okay? She said she wasn't feeling well when I talked to her this morning."

Danica let three more arrows loose, dropping two of the creatures before replying. "It was more like Penny was attacking Missy. I've never seen her that vicious before. She almost killed Missy outright, but the fight pulled the anti-magic bracelets off Missy, allowing her to portal out. But she was close to death when she left."

Finn slammed a shoulder into a charging Rougarou that Mila hadn't seen rushing into her blind spot. Remmy appeared and slit its throat before vanishing again.

Mila saw a new void portal open and couldn't believe her eyes when Missy stepped through while chugging a healing potion. She was blood-covered and looked like someone had thrown her into a blender face-first. The healing potion kicked in immediately, or more than likely it was the second one she had drank. Every step she took saw more of her flesh knitting back together—everything except the angry scorched eye socket. That stayed empty .

Missy's wings burst from her back, their top half still black and trailing down to golden at the feather tips. She flexed her back and rolled her shoulders with her silver sword gripped tight in her hand.

Seeing the blade reminded Mila that they hadn't picked it up after the fight in the street. She frowned at the stupid move and squared off with the approaching fallen Valkyrie.

"I knew that stupid crispy bitch would find a way to you. She's not nearly as defeated as Azoth thinks, but he's already written her off. Not me. No, I had a thrall keep an eye on her. Even those empty husks can use a tracking stone." Missy swung her sword in a series of windmilling chops, warming up her still-healing arms. "Let me guess, she tricked you into coming then sent the pack after you? She should have learned that she needs to be a little more hands-on with you."

Missy lunged the last ten feet and brought her sword around in a wide arc, her snarling face screaming with bloodlust.

Mila powered up a shield and hunkered down, gritting her teeth, ready to take the wild swing before countering. But the hit never came.

Mila looked up to see that a portal had opened behind Missy, and a long black and purple tentacle had reached through the blackness and wrapped itself around Missy's waist.

The battlefield suddenly went quiet as the Rougarou stopped attacking. They crouched into defensive positions and slowly backed away from the four of them.

Missy screamed in rage, kicking her feet in the air as the appendage lifted her two feet off the sand. She seemed to consider chopping the tentacle, but before she could act, it pulled her body violently pulled backward and through the portal.

Portals opened behind each of the remaining Rougarou, and they quickly vanished into them before they closed. Soon, the only portal remaining was the one Missy had disappeared into.

After a second's silence, Azoth stepped out of it. Mila felt the thick dark power radiating off him that left a metallic taste in her mouth. The difference in his power levels compared to the last time they had stood this close to one another was night and day. This was a Drude at its full strength. If she hadn't grown in her power, she feared that his presence would have driven her to her knees.

He stood tall, the sleeves of his robe hanging at his sides hiding his arms and any weapons he might be holding. The stance made Mila wonder if he'd regrown the arm she'd chopped off or if he was hiding the deformity from her.

His hood slowly swiveled, taking in the carnage sprawled across the sands, until the infinite black void that passed for his face stopped on Mila.

"Two days, little Valkyrie," he said in that voice that sounded like a thousand rusty hinges all groaning at once. "I should have let Yaminah continue her ploy. Perhaps she would have coaxed the Reaper's location from you. Until she reported back, I thought she had been trying to escape.

Missy, on the other hand… I may have broken her a little more than I had originally intended. Her mind… Well, you understand."

"Oh, I understand all right." Mila's face was a mask of disgusted anger. "You're a sick fuck who doesn't understand how to control his minions."

Azoth stared at her, not moving a muscle, for long enough that it became awkward.

"Two days. If you do not bring me the Reaper, I shall unleash a plague of death and destruction across this broken-down ship that will leave billions dead and the rest wishing to join them. Their fate is in your hands, little one. Make the right choice."

He turned and started toward his portal, the sand he crossed looking like a thousand snakes had been writhing in a ball across its surface.

"Does that mean you're calling off your dogs until we meet in two days?" Mila wanted to know where they stood as far as random attacks went.

Azoth laughed, a truly hideous sound. "I will not make it so easy for you. I made promises to my minions and will reward them greatly if they can bring me the weapon early. But, be warned that if you do not freely give me the Reaper, then I shall unleash my army to burn this all to the ground. Think of it as a fun little game of keep away." He paused, then turned to look over his shoulder at her. "So you know I'm serious, you might want to look into the missing people."

Then he stepped through the portal and disappeared.

"What an asshole." Remmy wiped the blood off her daggers on the fur of a dead Rougarou.

"A powerful asshole," Danica retorted.

Mila put the Ivar back in its holster. "Powerful or not, his days are numbered."

"Only if the untested device works."

Mila clenched her jaw while staring through the space where the portal had been. "It'll work." A frown grew on her face, and in a much quieter voice she added, "it has to work."

CHAPTER SEVENTEEN

They teleported back to the condo after Finn did a little earth magic to make the bodies and blood sink deep into the sand. The last thing they wanted was to have the Feds looking into two dozen butchered wolfmen found in a national park.

As soon as they appeared, Mila went straight to Victoria who was lying on her stomach on the floor. Her bloodstained shirt had been removed and was in a wad in the center of an alarmingly large pool of her blood.

Mila saw that the stab wound in the center of her back had mostly closed, but blood was still slowly oozing from it.

"How are you doing, Victoria?" Mila knelt beside the elder Valkyrie and put a comforting hand on her bare shoulder.

Victoria groaned and turned her head to face Mila, although she kept her eyes closed. "I've been better. I can feel the potion trying to heal the last of the wound, but something is keeping it from happening."

"Danica, toss me one of the gym towels, would you?"

Danica went over to the towel cart they kept in the dojo, grabbed one of the small hand towels, and tossed it to Mila.

After snatching the towel out of the air, Mila wiped away the blood to get a better look at the wound. Leaning in, she pulled the towel over the split skin, making Victoria wince. "Sorry." She patted Victoria's back but swiped again to clear the fresh blood.

Mila saw black rot around the wound's edges and growled. "That bitch. She somehow channeled some infernal magic into the wound, which means the anti-magic bracelets still need a little work."

"Fuck." Victoria weakly pounded a fist on the floor. "I was afraid of that. This will take weeks to heal. There's no way I can be at a hundred percent in two days."

"I think I can get it out. Give me a minute."

Victoria twisted her head so she could frown up at Mila. "You can't do that. It's not how this works."

"I've been doing it since back in Idaho." Mila raised an eyebrow. "It's not all that hard. You only need to flush it out with celestial magic."

"You can't put your magic into something. That was the whole point when we were talking to Rebecca about the fundamental differences between a Drude and a Valkyrie. We can channel our power into spells, or use it to reinforce our bodies, but you can't take raw magic and move it someplace else."

Mila sat back and cocked her head at Victoria. "That's exactly what we've been doing when we charge the device."

Snorting, then wincing in pain, Victoria shook her

head. "No, that's the genius of the device. We aren't putting power into it. It's taking power from us. That's why it drains you so completely. It goes until you only have so much left then it stops before it kills you."

Mila didn't do that. She chose how much power the device got because she was the one charging it, not the other way around. No wonder Victoria dreaded using it—having to trust that the device didn't accidentally kill you every time must have been terrifying.

Mila decided it was better to show than tell in this instance. She reached out with her power tentacle and probed Victoria's back until she felt the infernal infection. In a quick but forceful move, she stabbed into the wound with her power.

Victoria clenched up, her arms pulling in under her chest and her legs drawing up to lift her butt and lower back into the air. Golden and black sparks shot out of the wound in a violent spray that crackled into nothingness before they hit the floor.

It only took a second, but Victoria stayed clenched for a good thirty seconds after the magic was expelled. Mila watched as the healing potion finally finished its work and closed the wound, leaving perfectly smooth and pink skin across her spine.

Victoria finally relaxed and fell back to the floor. She was breathing hard, but reached a hand to her back and felt around with probing fingers.

"What the hell was that?"

"I told you it was easy." Mila rocked back onto her heels and stood. She turned and headed for Penny's room, wanting to check on her friend before she got into a lengthy debate with Victoria about what was and wasn't possible.

Finn fell in beside her as she crossed the dojo. "You did good out there today."

She smiled up at him and knocked on Penny's small door. "Thanks. I had a pretty great teacher."

He chuckled, then reached for the handle of the large door and turned the knob.

"Uh, shouldn't we give her a second to answer before we barge in?" Mila pulled him back from the door before he could walk in.

"I'm pretty sure she won't answer." He pulled her to the door and opened it.

Mila's breath caught in her throat when she spotted Penny wrapped around her three eggs. "Why didn't she say anything?"

"It's part of the whole mystery thing. For whatever reason, faerie dragons are driven to give birth isolated from their friends and family. She warned me about it years ago." He was looking down at Penny with a warm smile nestled in his thick beard.

Glancing up at the wall above the hoard pile, Mila raised an eyebrow at the message burned into the paint like a brand.

"Well, you don't see that every day." Finn laughed. "At least she let us know what's happening."

The message was simple. "Sorry, Danica. Love you too. I'll be out for at least a week recovering. Don't bother trying to wake me. It won't work."

"Well, shit." Mila crossed her arms. "We'll have to teleport the whole hoard, then."

"Are we going somewhere?"

"Well, we can't stay here. Missy more than likely figured out where the building is by looking out the windows during her short and violent stay. You heard Azoth—he's encouraging them to come after us. This is why we set up the second location at Rebecca's."

Finn nodded, pulled Penny's door closed, and headed back out into the living room. Mila followed, recognizing his decisions face. He was about to get shit done. It always gave Mila the chills to see him in his element.

Danica had found a t-shirt for Victoria, who was leaning on the back of the couch, her face still full of confused wonder.

"Remmy," Finn's tone was confident, "I need you to tell everyone we're evacuating the building. They have an hour to pack up what they need for a few days, a week at most. Then we need to empty the building. Have them go to Christine's if they don't have anywhere else to go. Grab a few things for yourself, and meet us here when you're done."

Remmy gave him a sharp salute. "Got it, boss," she replied without any humor. She knew Finn's serious voice and headed for the door at a jog.

"Danica, we need to teleport Penny and her entire hoard in one go."

Danica blanched, her eyes growing wide. "I don't think I can do that. That's literally tons of gold in there."

"You can do it, but you'll need a little help. You and I will head over to Rebecca's and Lance's to get things ready. In the meantime, Mila, you and Victoria pack some things for the rest of us while we're getting things ready for

Penny. Keep your guard up. I think we have at least a few hours before Missy will try anything, but it never hurts to be ready. If she shows up, you two need to lead her on a nice long chase to get her away from Penny. In her current state, she's completely defenseless."

Mila nodded and glanced over her shoulder at Penny's door, still not believing they would have baby dragons running around in no time. "We'll be sure to keep her safe."

"Okay, Danica. Let's go." Finn leaned down and kissed Mila before stepping close to Danica, who formed a bubble. Then they vanished.

"What the hell happened to Finn?" Victoria looked at the spot he and Danica had been standing. "He's usually so laid back, but that was...intense. He sounded like a commander or something."

Mila smiled. "He *is* a dwarf king, you know. That part isn't a joke."

"I can see that."

CHAPTER EIGHTEEN

"I don't know what's happening with you, but it's not normal." Victoria stuffed a handful of random underwear and socks from Danica's dresser into a duffel bag.

They were packing fast, not choosing outfits as much as covering the essentials by grabbing something for the top, the bottom, and the undercarriage. Danica was going to hate that it didn't all go together. Feeling a little guilty, Mila at least made sure to grab Danica's favorite shirt and leggings from a drawer before sliding it closed.

"I'm a new Valkyrie. You're the one who told me I would develop new abilities. Now that I have, you're telling me it's not natural?" Mila selected a pair of black sneakers and a pair of leather boots and stuffed them into the bag as well. Knowing her friend better than anyone else on the planet, Mila also grabbed a pair of black high-heeled booties, then went to the closet and picked a red sheath dress and a black skater dress, tucking them into the bag before moving to the bathroom.

"Yes, new abilities, not *impossibilities*." She gave Mila a knowing look. "You're a smart woman, Mila. You know something is strange."

Staring at the bathroom counter covered in a hundred beauty products, Mila only had the most basic understanding of their intended use. She considered taking them all since she didn't know what Danica would want. But in the end, she decided to keep it simple with a brush, toothbrush, eyeliner and mascara. They were the four things Mila used every day, and she wasn't getting any complaints. Danica would have to rough it.

Zipping up the stuffed bag, Mila turned to Victoria. The older woman was giving her a questioning look, her arms crossed and blocking the door.

Rolling her eyes, Mila sighed dramatically. "Fine. You're right. I know there's more going on than there should be. But what am I supposed to do about it? It's happening whether I like it or not."

Victoria smiled and stepped back, allowing Mila to pass. "I'm not saying we need to stop it. I'm saying we need to understand it. I can only teach you how to do things that, at the very least, are similar to what I already know how to do. I can't teach you how to channel your raw power into something else. I don't even have a reference point to start from."

Victoria followed Mila into the living room, where she dropped the duffel and headed for Penny's room. "So, what are you suggesting?"

"It's pretty obvious that Rebecca thinks you're taking on some of Finn's traits, and I have to agree. Maybe there's something there you can use against Azoth, but we don't know enough to try something."

Mila quietly opened Penny's door and peeked in to check on her. She hadn't moved a muscle since Mila had first seen her.

"I'll see what Finn thinks," Mila conceded. "To be honest with you, I think you and Rebecca are onto something. Finn told me that calling down lightning like I did is an ability that the Shield Maidens have passed to them by the Emperor. I think Finn has a little more authority than he thinks he does."

Victoria's brows rose slowly as the implications dawned on her, but the popping sound of Finn and Danica returning interrupted her reply.

Mila stepped around Victoria and saw that they had brought along guests. Rebecca and Lance stood beside Finn, Lance in a polo and cargo shorts, and Rebecca in a bikini with a thin robe wrapped around herself.

"Do you ever wear real clothes? I feel like you're always in some sort of swimwear." Mila smiled as she stepped up and hugged the blue-haired woman.

"Oh, darling, why would I wear anything but the bare minimum? It's not like we have any neighbors spying on us." She returned the hug. "I hear you're going to be an aunt. Congratulations."

Mila chuckled. "I guess I am. What are you two doing here?"

"They're going to help Danica teleport Penny and her hoard." Finn led them all over to Penny's room and pushed the door open. "They'll be able to supplement Danica's magic with theirs," he whispered.

"Why didn't you have Victoria and I do that?"

"Because we have an entirely different kind of magic.

Celestial magic doesn't mix well with others," Victoria answered. "Not to mention we can't give our magic to others, at least most of us can't." She gave Mila a knowing look.

"Did you get everything packed up?" Danica stepped into Penny's room and sized up the pile of gold.

"Yeah, it's in the duffel." Mila pointed to the bag in the living room. "We should move soon. It's been an hour, and Remmy texted a few minutes ago to let me know she got everyone out of the building. She'll be up once she's packed her bag."

Rebecca and Lance stepped up behind Danica and put a hand each on her shoulders. Finn came up behind them and put a hand on Lance's shoulder.

"Okay, this is pretty simple," Finn explained to the group. "For most races, you three included, magic is limitless but has restricted flow. One person can only direct so much power through themselves, but if we channel our power through Danica, then she can control that much more. She's going to need a crap ton of power to get all this treasure in one teleport, so be sure to give her all she needs. But, be careful not to give her too much, or it can cause her some real damage. Let her take what she needs since she'll have a much better feel for how much that is."

He glanced around to be sure everyone understood the instructions and got a round of nods from everyone.

"Okay. Danica, you have the wheel."

Mila stepped back to be sure she could see the whole show.

Danica started by forming a large bubble that encircled the entire hoard, the light of the single desk lamp in the room reflecting off its surface. When she had given all she could to the spell, Mila saw that the surface of the bubble was still quite thin compared to when she teleported them around.

"Okay, I'm going to draw power," Danica warned.

Lance's hand glowed, followed a second later by Rebecca's hand, then Finn's. Mila watched as the power flowed into Danica with enough strength that Mila could see it. A mist-like haze rose from the elf's shoulders as she closed her eyes and flexed long fingers that crackled with power.

The bubble thickened, and its surface gained the iridescence Mila was used to seeing. It looked like everything was going to plan as the bubble continued to solidify. Then it suddenly stopped, and Danica grunted with effort.

"I need a little more," she said through gritted teeth.

"I'm giving you everything I have," Rebecca replied, followed by a "Me too," from Lance.

"That's it from me as well," Finn rumbled, his eyes narrowed in concentration.

"I only need a little more. It's so close." The frustration in Danica's voice was clear, but there didn't seem to be anything she could do about it.

Mila stepped forward, wondering if maybe she could somehow convert her celestial magic. Azoth could do it, so why not her? She already showed abilities similar to the Drude, so perhaps this was one of those things Victoria was talking about. Mila could already push her magic into things, which Victoria had said was impossible. This was only taking that one step further, right?

Mila took another step and reached for Finn's shoulder. The click of the front door opening then latching closed made Mila look toward the kitchen. Remmy walked down the hall, a backpack on her shoulders. She was whistling the tune of a popular song on the radio and didn't seem to have a care in the world.

"Remmy!" Finn shouted, making Mila jump back, her hand dropping to her side.

"What's up, boss?" Remmy came around the corner and saw them all struggling with the spell. Her eyes went wide, and she dropped the pack to the ground as she ran up to Rebecca and pressed a hand to her back.

A green glow flowed from Remmy, dimmer than the rest of them, but still enough that Mila could see it. The pained look of concentration on Danica's face relaxed, and with the added power, the bubble snapped into existence around Penny and her nest of treasure.

Danica's shoulders slumped as she breathed out a long breath she had been inadvertently holding. "That was intense." She chuckled, rolled her shoulders, and smiled over her shoulder at her helpers. "Thanks for the save, Remmy."

"No problem, simply doing my part." Remmy tossed her long white braid over her shoulder. "We blowing this tooter stand or what?"

Danica laughed. "Yeah. You want to come with Penny and me?"

Remmy snatched up her bag and shrugged it onto her shoulders. "Sure. Might as well be a part of the most expensive teleport in history. Has anyone figured out how much all this treasure is worth?"

Mila raised an eyebrow. "Actually, no. There must be quite a few tons of gold alone. But to be honest, those gems might be worth more than the gold. That ruby is bigger than my fist." She pointed out a particularly bright red stone half-buried in the coins.

"Right now, it's worth more than your life if you try and mess with it," Finn warned. "Penny might be sleeping now, but you mess with her hoard and she'll bite your face off before she's fully awake. I recommend you don't touch anything during the trip."

Remmy stuck her hands in the pockets of her leather bodysuit and stepped close to Danica, who had already taken her position in the large bubble.

"Good call." Finn chuckled.

"See you in a few minutes." Danica waved.

The bubble popped.

Instead of the quiet noise that normally came from the teleport spell activating, this time it sounded like a bolt of lightning had struck the building. Everyone stumbled back from the concussive blast as dust rained down from unseen cracks in the ceiling.

"Holy shit, I did not expect that," Mila shouted, her voice sounding muffled in her ears.

"What?" Rebecca shouted, but only sounding like a whisper to Mila.

"I didn't expect that!"

"I don't know how they made cars."

"What?"

"What?" Rebecca retorted, completely lost.

Finn rolled his eyes, walked over to the duffel bag, and began digging through it. A second later, he stood holding five healing potions from the box Mila had packed earlier.

He passed them out and indicated that they should all drink.

Mila thought it was a bit much for something that would eventually fade on its own. That was until she saw a trickle of blood run down Rebecca's cheek from her ear.

When she pressed a hand to her ear, it surprised Mila to see her fingers come away with blood on them. She drank the potion.

Ten minutes later, they were all standing close to Lance who created a teleport bubble around them.

"What was that about cars?" Mila looked up at Rebecca.

"What?"

"Not this again," Finn sighed.

The bubble popped, leaving the condo empty.

CHAPTER NINETEEN

The hallway cutting through the center of Rebecca's house had grown since they were last there a day and a half ago. Instead of two guest bedrooms, there were now four rooms total—three bedrooms and one thick-walled, reinforced chamber that currently held several tons of treasure, one faerie dragon, and three eggs.

The only decoration in the room was the floor-to-ceiling window that made up the entire wall opposite the door. The view looked west, out across the strangely beautiful bayou. Over the last hour, Mila had watched the sun fall closer and closer to the canopy of cypress trees spread out below the suspended house. Now she half-watched as the sun's orange orb finally set in earnest. The sky slowly changed from a crystal-clear blue to a warm orange color that continued to darken while Mila watched. As if by magic, the orange changed to purples and pinks that streaked across the horizon in a final show of beauty before the last of the sun disappeared, marking one more day gone.

It had taken Mila an embarrassingly long time to realize that the view was impossible. At least, it was impossible if she weren't standing in a semi-sentient house that used magic to rearrange itself in the blink of an eye.

The room was in the center of the house. Rebecca's and Lance's bedroom suite should have been where the window looked out on the bayou. Not to mention the wall faced south, not west. But Mila didn't sweat the small stuff like cardinal direction and physical walls anymore. She had seen too much, become too much, and done too much for it to bother her.

Now, she simply appreciated the view.

Mila leaned against the doorframe of Penny's room, her arms crossed, lost in thought about what exactly she would do in the coming battle. She watched Penny's chest rise and fall in slow, methodical breaths. Once in a while, a puff of flame from one or the other of her nostrils punctuated the calm. Each puff created a tiny smoke ring that would steadily rise until it broke across the dark gray ceiling. Twitching tremors occasionally ran down Penny's spine, letting Mila know that she was dreaming while in that coma-like sleep. Mila couldn't decide if that would be a good thing or not. With a small shrug and a half-smile, she decided it all depended on what the dream was about.

Not for the first time in the last hour, Mila wished that Penny was awake. She could use her advice on how to plan out the coming battle. Penny was their strategist, the brains of their little trio. Without her, they were a little like the straw man from Oz—full of good intentions, but more than likely being taken apart by crows.

Normally, Mila wouldn't worry too much. She and

Finn were smart, capable people after all, and she knew they could get through most situations without much trouble, even if they made mistakes. But, this time was different. This time, they were betting the lives of billions that they could take Azoth down.

To make matters worse, this wasn't the same Azoth she'd faced before. This Azoth was more powerful than he'd ever been, even in the first battle with the Valkyries.

But that wasn't the only question she wrestled with.

There was the question of the device working as it was designed to do. So far, it did exactly what it should—it stored power like a champ. But, she had to remind herself that it was designed by a witch who had only seen a Drude once and got most of his information from a single Valkyrie, and one that was currently the slave of that same Drude.

Gregory was obviously a genius, but even they were wrong from time to time. Would the device discharge fast enough? Were the hundreds of charges enough to wipe out Azoth's stored power, or were they vastly underestimating him? How close did she have to be to activate the device?

She had decided that she would use the most obvious answers to those questions. She had to trust that the device had sufficient flow. It would have as many charges as they could pack into it in the time they had left. And she was planning on activating the thing as close to the Drude as possible.

Was that enough to bet the human race on success?

Mila shook her head, trying to banish the doubt. She didn't have a choice but to move ahead with the scraps of a plan. What was at stake was far bigger than this planet. If the Drude got their hands on the Reaper, they would be able to permanently shift the balance of power in their direction. They would become unstoppable, crashing over the universe like a tsunami and leaving nothing in their wake. That would never happen if Mila had anything to say about it.

Looking up, Mila realized how long she had been standing there, lost in thought. The sun was well below the horizon, and the constant chirp of the peepers had taken on a more subdued pace with the veil of night blanketing the endless stretches of swamp.

A tiny puff of flame lit the room in warm light for a heartbeat, drawing Mila's attention to her friend curled around her newborns. A smile spread across her lips as she watched Penny sleep.

Mila spoke quietly to the sleeping dragon. "I could use your help, Penny. This is a big one, and there might be too many variables for me to see it all. If you think of anything we might have missed, let me know, would ya?"

Another puff of flame that left a rising smoke ring was the only reply.

Mila pushed off the doorframe and smoothed down the front of the black skater dress she wore before turning and heading down the hall. Her bare feet padding down the hardwood floor barely made a noise as she headed toward the sounds of sizzling food and friendly conversation.

She had grabbed the skater dress from Danica's closet, intending it for the elf, but after a quick shower, Mila had realized that she only brought jeans and her leather pants along. She felt like wearing something light and breezy while she had the time to relax before the confrontation with Azoth. So she pulled the dress out of the duffel and put it on without a second thought.

The truth was that the dress belonged to both of them, as did most of the dresses in their closets. When one of them bought a dress or top, both assumed that they would wear it at some point. No one would ever guess that they shared so many clothes after looking at the two women standing next to one another. Danica was more than a foot taller than Mila's 4'10", but all of that extra height was in her long legs. They had remarkably similar body measurements, as long as you excluded their legs. Mila's chest was smaller than Danica's, but it wasn't such a big difference that it changed the actual size of the clothes. So, while the light cotton dress came to just over Mila's knee, it only covered a third of Danica's shapely thighs, giving them a vastly different look from the same dress.

It was a little like the difference between Danica and herself. They knew each other better than any two people had any right to. And when you stripped away everything but the core of who they were, you found two people who were more similar than anyone suspected. Both of them were nerds for their chosen fields, read scientific articles for fun, and talked endlessly about some new technique in their field that would bore anyone else to tears. But they would sit and listen to one another ramble off technical details and be as excited about each other's discovery as they would be about their own.

They both were slow to trust but fiercely loyal once they did. They loved the same dorky movies and nineties trivia and Harry Potter. Rarely did they disagree on what to eat, or watch, or do for fun. But while they were basically the same person on the inside, much like the black dress, they were seen as vastly different from the outside. Danica made the dress look sexy and flirty, showing off long toned legs for the world to see, while Mila made the dress look cute and modest, the focus on how the cuffed sleeves framed her shoulders and head while drawing attention to her long black hair.

It was the same dress, but no one ever noticed that they both wore it.

As she came around the corner, Mila saw Lance, Finn, and Victoria working on dinner in the kitchen. Finn was preparing a large salad while Victoria mashed a large bowl of creamy potatoes, and Lance was busy searing up shrimp in a huge stainless-steel pan while a full platter of giant scallops sat on the counter awaiting their turn in the herbed brown butter.

Danica and Rebecca sat with their chairs at the dining table turned toward the clear glass wall, sipping steaming cups of something and watching Remmy as she played with Grimm out in the pool.

The sun had set and night had truly fallen, but the patio was still lit by a warm magical light that, while not coming from anywhere, still glowed everywhere.

Everyone was laughing and having a great time in each other's company, thoughts of the coming battle forgotten for the night. Mila felt guilty for taking it easy while Azoth did who knew what in preparation for their confrontation. But logically, she knew there was nothing they could do but wait. There was no need to worry about the things she couldn't change.

She had considered using the cube Yaminah had given

her, but she was still nervous that it might let the Drude track her to Rebecca's house, and she wasn't willing to put them in danger. Besides, it wasn't like the cube told them where he was. They would have to recognize the place to find him, and the image Yaminah had first shown her had been a dark room with a throne. It could have been anywhere.

Mila walked up behind Danica and leaned over, planting a kiss on the top of her head before taking the chair beside her at the table.

"What was that for?" Danica touched the spot Mila had kissed in surprise.

Mila shrugged. "I was thinking about you. You're a good friend, Danica. You don't have to fight this battle, you know. It's not your fight."

Danica rolled her eyes as she lifted her leg and playfully pushed Mila's knee. "I know that. But you would be right there next to me in the same circumstances. Don't worry about me. I know exactly what I'm getting into and why I'm doing it."

Finn came over and set a steaming cup on the table in front of Mila, then winked at her. "Rebecca, did you tell Mila about what you found? It might make her feel a little better."

"I was about to, pushy. Give a girl a second to settle in." Rebecca sounded like a big sister.

Finn held up his hands in mock surrender and backed away.

Mila laughed at the ridiculous display and turned to Rebecca. "What's he talking about?"

"I did a little more reading after you left. When you said

the device had three hundred charges or more, that didn't sit right with me. Gregory was a hell of a documentarian, but sometimes I think he wrote faster than his brain could keep up.

"When he said it should hold twenty or so charges, he meant it should *take* twenty or more charges. He was estimating the minimum."

Mila sipped from the mug, surprised to find hot cider with a healthy dose of spiced rum mixed in. She took another large swallow, savoring the flavor before replying.

"So, did you find out what the device's capacity is?"

Rebecca chuckled. "It's infinite."

"Infinite? How is that possible?"

"So, Old Greg as Victoria likes to call him, was a rather clever bastard. He took the same principles the Drude use to store their power and created a device to mimic that ability."

Victoria held up the device after pulling it from a pocket, having heard the conversation from the kitchen. "It's a pocket dimension." She tossed the brass-colored ball over the island to Mila.

Catching the heavy multi-segmented sphere, Mila looked at it with new appreciation. "There's another dimension in here? Like a different universe?"

"Not exactly." Rebecca waggled her hands in a "sort of" motion. "It's a pocket dimension. Think of it as an empty plot of land. You could build a universe on it, but right now there's nothing there. It's empty."

"But it's infinite?"

Danica nodded. "Yeah, but it's a small infinite. Like

from calculus—it's infinite but less infinite than other infinities."

Mila groaned. "God, I hated calculus. But I think I hate that I understand what you mean, which is thanks to that sadistic class, even more. We can put power into it forever and never fill it, but it's not big enough that we could fit everything in it, because it's smaller than this universe. It's part of this universe, unlike the place the Drude keeps its power, which is somewhere else entirely."

"Exactly." Danica laughed. "It's a pocket dimension."

"So, long story short, we can't overload this thing and blow it up by accident."

"Nope," Rebecca confirmed.

"Good." Mila closed her eyes and forced another charge into the device. She pushed the power as hard as she could, trying to see how much flow she could get into it. There was a definite bottleneck, but she'd drained herself down to her last ten percent and opened her eyes before the scallops were plated. It was far faster than she'd ever done it before, and she took a large gulp of the hot cider as a reward, finishing off the mug.

She put the device on the table and held her mug over her head. In her best Viking impression, she shouted, "Another!"

Danica's eyes went wide. "You drank that already? How? Mine is practically still boiling, and I got it ten minutes before you did."

Mila looked at her in confusion. The cider was hot, but it wasn't *that* hot. She looked over to see Finn take a big gulp from his steaming cup before starting to chop the cucumbers for the salad.

"Well, I guess that answers that, then." Mila lowered the mug. "I'm becoming a dwarf, aren't I?"

Rebecca nodded. "Yeah. Well, partly. You're still a Valkyrie, but you're also becoming something else. Your new Valkyrie status doesn't account for this much change, though. There's something else working on you as well."

"Yeah, but what?"

"I have a theory, but…it's a little far-fetched." Rebecca hedged.

Mila laughed. "More far-fetched than me changing species?"

"Good point." She leaned in and gave Mila a long appraising look before continuing. "Have you ever heard of the Elementals?"

To Rebecca's obvious surprise, both Mila and Danica nodded.

"You have?" She leaned back and looked them over as if trying to judge whether they were telling the truth. "Are you fucking with me?"

Mila laughed and shook her head. "I did a little job with Dirt a couple of months ago. Nice guy, not very talkative though. Are there others?"

It took Rebecca a few seconds to recover. "You're for sure going to have to tell me about that sometime, but to answer the question, yes there are others. No one but the Huldu knows who they are, but that's not the important part. The important thing is that the Elementals were a reaction by *Earth* herself. She needed to protect something precious, so she intervened, and the Elementals were born."

Mila raised an eyebrow as she regarded Rebecca.

"You're saying *Earth* is aware and created a race of dirt people to protect something?"

Rebecca shook her head while frowning. "What? No. Sorry, I didn't explain that very well. Yes, *Earth* is somewhat sentient. It was a feature of the great ship that made it so advanced. No, she did not create a race of dirt men. All the Elementals are of different races. But, she did *modify* them. Much in the same way you're changing. It's only a theory."

"Hypothesis," Mila and Danica said at the same time.

"What?"

"Never mind." Mila waved away the comment. "Why would *Earth* need me to become something different?"

Rebecca shrugged, but Finn and Lance came in with steaming dishes of food followed by Victoria with the large salad Finn had made before Mila could ask any more. Not that she knew what to ask anyway.

CHAPTER TWENTY

That night, Mila laid in the crook of Finn's arm, the covers thrown off the bed once again as they let the conditioned air evaporate the sweat from their bodies. Mila was still breathing heavily, trying to catch her breath.

"You okay over there, darlin'? You're huffing like the oxygen scrubbers went out on your ship," Finn commented in an infuriatingly not-out-of-breath way.

Mila tried to blow a strand of sweat-soaked hair from her face, but it refused to budge. Huffing in slight frustration, she sat up and spun around to sit cross-legged on the bed beside Finn. She quickly gathered her hair in both hands and twisted it into a large sloppy bun on the top of her head and held it there with one hand as she fanned her face with her free one.

"Sorry, babe. You're way too hot to lay against right now."

Finn got a goofy grin on his face and waved the comment away with comical awkwardness. "Awe, thanks, babe. You're not so bad yourself."

She lightly slapped his abdomen, getting a satisfying "Oof!" from him.

She rolled her eyes and chuckled. "You're such a dork. You know what I mean."

He chuckled along with her. "Yeah, I know. What I want to know is if you're feeling okay. Usually, you're pulling blankets off the floor within two minutes of finishing."

Mila felt a bead of sweat roll out of the back of her hair and down her back, while at the same time she saw that Finn was already dry and relaxed. Even his chest hair was standing back up in curly tufts. Was she okay?

"I think so. I'm not cooling down. Maybe all that hot cider is finally catching up with me."

Finn rolled out of bed and walked to the bathroom, disappearing behind the door but leaving it half-open. The faucet turned on for a few seconds then Finn came back out, folding a damp towel into a four-inch-wide long strip. He came over to the bed and reached around her neck, then draped the cold towel over it so the ends hung against her chest.

She stiffened at the sudden chill but quickly felt relief as her body finally started to cool down.

"Oh, that's amazing."

Finn grinned and fell back onto the bed, crossing his ankles as he bounced slightly before settling back into his spot. "Works every time."

They sat quietly, him laying back watching her while she kept her hair up and let out little moans of pleasure.

"How are things going with getting your berserker rage under control? Are you still talking with Rolf?" Mila asked out of nowhere.

Finn pursed his lips and folded his hands behind his head. "I see him fairly regularly. We usually grab lunch while I'm out in the afternoons. The training, if that's what you want to call it, is pretty much over. I can keep myself in the flow while still being able to cast."

"Are you still immune to magic while in the rage?"

"For the most part. I need to lose myself, though, if I want full immunity. At that point, I might as well be a wild animal so I can't go that far, but I can shrug off about eighty or ninety percent of a spell without much of a problem. Why?"

Mila bit her lip and gave him a coy look. "Do you think you could shrug off infernal magic?"

His face fell slightly. "Oh, that's why." He reached down and scratched his thigh while he thought about it. "I don't know. Maybe. The problem is that infernal is an entirely different kind of magic, but it's still a kind of magic. I honestly don't know. I do know that I don't want to find out, if at all possible."

Mila sighed, then pulled the damp towel from her neck and tossed it on the nightstand. "Well, there goes that plan. On to the next one, I guess." She swung her leg over him and settled down on his stomach.

His eyes brightened. "Oh, I like this plan, but it seems a lot like the one that nearly sent you into a full-on inferno. You sure?"

"We might not have much more time to do this before the big day. I want to get in some overtime." She smiled, her eyes sparkling with mischief. "Besides, you said your towel trick always works, right? I'm going to test that theory."

"You've been aggressive lately." He gave her a narrow-eyed look. "I like it."

She shrugged theatrically. "What can I say? I'm a stone-cold Manther killer."

Mila sipped her orange juice, washing down her second helping of bacon pancakes as everyone else was finishing up their first. Everyone but Finn, who was halfway through his third stack.

This whole dwarf thing was freaking Mila out a little. She couldn't remember eating that much for breakfast in a long time. What scared her was that she wanted another pancake.

"You were so right, Finn. These are amazing." Lance took another bite and chewed with a big smile on his face.

"Yeah, they're really good!" Grimm echoed, bouncing in his seat while he stabbed another bite onto his fork.

Finn leaned back while taking a long pull of coffee and smiling. "The secret is mixing the salty and sweet. It's an entire culinary style on my homeworld."

Rebecca wiped the corner of her mouth and picked up her juice glass. "I'm pretty sure that's a well-known combination here on *Earth*, too."

Finn's face fell a little, but he shrugged it off. "I should have guessed. There were dwarves here in the beginning, after all. Probably got passed down through the generations."

"That might be what happened." Rebecca winked at Mila.

Mila snorted a laugh, then cleared her throat and asked the first thing that came to mind so she didn't have to answer the suspicious look Finn gave her. "Have any of you heard about people disappearing?"

She wasn't sure why she asked that until she remembered it was what Azoth told her to look into, to see that he was serious. Suddenly, she cared about what the answer might be.

Everyone shook their heads while looking at her like she had an ear growing out of her forehead.

"It's funny you should ask that." Lance swallowed his last bite quickly. "I was on a forum this morning where they were talking about villages around the world vanishing off the map."

Rebecca groaned and reached over to pat him on the arm. "Babe, please tell me you're not talking about those conspiracy forums."

He laughed and nodded. "Yeah, I am." He turned to the rest of them to explain. "We research magical people and creatures like her family has done for as long as anyone can remember. As you can probably guess, by this point, there isn't much the family hasn't found and written about extensively. We'll have to show you guys the library at some point. It's insane. There are literally tens of thousands of books dating all the way back to before *Earth* was even in the design process."

"Babe." Rebecca gently knocked him out of his tangent.

"Right, sorry about that. I love that damned library. I'll be honest, I can't believe the family entrusted the collection to us. Especially since it took so much convincing to get the Huldu to unpack Gregory's shipping crate. He brought copies of everything he could get his hands on before booking passage…" Lance got a distant look on his face as he began heading to his beloved library in his mind.

"Babe," Rebecca repeated, this time a little louder.

Lance shook his head, clearing whatever had taken his thoughts. "Sorry."

Mila laughed, her shoulders shaking slightly. "It's fine. I get passionate about my interests, too."

"I bet. Anthropology is fascinating. It's a large part of what we do. Maybe we could collaborate at some point. Having an expert would speed things up considerably."

Mila considered Lance's proposal. She didn't know if she would ever go back to the museum at this point. Maybe working with him and Rebecca would be nice.

"I'll consider it." Mila waved for him to continue. "You were saying about the forum?"

"Yes, conspiracy forums are ninety percent insane people shouting into an echo chamber, but once in a while, you find a real nugget. I started using them with the idea that there are still quite a few creatures from private collections in stasis down in the main storage hold. A lot of these creatures don't have any formal documentation on them. Now, stasis is a wonder of magic and technology, but it's not perfect. Once in a while, something gets loose and makes its way to the surface. More than likely it ends up on a conspiracy theory blog or forum. So, every morning I scan the threads and see if anything jumps out at me."

"And you found something on missing people?" Mila had no idea there were creatures held below *Earth*'s crust waiting to pop out and start eating people. It was fascinating. However, she'd fixated on the missing people.

Lance gave her a half-grin. "Not only people, whole towns. The people, the buildings, even the streets. Poof! Gone. So far, it's only been in remote places so no one has been able to corroborate the guy's story, but someone did the math and the numbers of missing from the towns the guy mentioned alone was over a hundred thousand. The huge number was enough that I wrote it off, but now that you're asking, I'm intrigued."

Mila frowned while thinking of the implications. She took a long drink of orange juice before replying. "It was something Azoth said at the dunes. Before he left, he said to look into the missing people so I would understand that he was serious. If he's stealing entire towns of people and making them into thralls, then he really will be able to start a world war."

"It's not possible," Victoria cut in. "Even if he's at full power, he wouldn't have nearly enough to turn them all into thralls. Thralls are magically cheap for him, but they still cost something, and that magic is separated from him so he can't replenish it unless he withdraws it, which kills the host. He can't convert numbers like that."

Rebecca opened the ever-present copy of Gregory's book and began flipping through the pages. "If I'm not mistaken, according to Missy, or whatever her name was back then, a Drude can control huge numbers of people, but only for a relatively short time." She scanned the page she had stopped on, and her eyes brightened when she was about halfway down. "Here it is. She said that it was a form of mind control. The Drude would cast the spell over a population, and they would be his for a few weeks. Evidently, they can't take complex orders, but simple things like attack, defend, run, etcetera were fine. But the important part is that the people weren't harmed when the spell wore off or someone broke it. If that's what he's using, then we can save those people. Kill him, and they're free."

Mila and Finn blew out long breaths and leaned back in their chairs. They made eye contact and traded the same concern.

"What?" Rebecca noted the concern on their faces. "This is a good thing. Those people don't end up as piles of cursed dust when that tentacled bastard drops dead."

"True, but…" Finn started, but his voice trailed off since he didn't want to say it.

Mila continued. "If we can save them, that means we can't kill them. Don't get me wrong, it's amazing that we get the chance to save them and don't have to write off a cities' worth of people, but it makes this infinitely harder. And I don't mean a small infinity. I'm talking one of the big ones—infinity plus one kinda stuff."

"We need to get help," Finn said.

"We do," Mila agreed, "but I don't want to call them in quite yet."

"Call who in?" Lance asked.

Danica smiled, but it was Remmy who answered. "Carl and the gang."

CHAPTER TWENTY-ONE

The plan was simple. Finn, Danica, and Remmy needed to hold off the masses of minions, while Victoria kept Missy occupied, and Mila hit Azoth with the device. Once it drained his power, Mila would kill him, setting Missy and Yaminah free along with however many people Azoth had under the mind control spell, and the minions would fall to dust with no power to sustain them. Bing, bang, boom, the whole thing would be over in less than a minute or two.

"I love you, darlin', but that's a shit plan." Finn had a painfully sad look on his face.

They had gathered in the living room and were sitting on couches and plush chairs. Mila stood in front of the open window wall, the morning breeze ruffling the skater dress she had put back on when she woke up. A white-board the house had made for her when her back was turned stood on an easel, the tray loaded with a rainbow of markers. She had written the main actions of the plan in black with bullet points in blue, simply because she could.

Grimm was blissfully unaware of what was going on as he sat between his parents,, big studio headphones covering his ears while he got lost in his game of *Cupcaction!*

"I'm well aware," Mila reassured him. "That's why we're brainstorming. The key points I see that need some serious thought are," she tapped the capped end of her marker on each item as she addressed it. "One. How do we keep the masses at bay with three people? Two. What is the backup plan if the device doesn't work? Three. What if the device does work, but it takes a long time?"

Victoria, having spent most of her current life in a boardroom, had no trouble quickly speaking up. "You need to add, 'How does Victoria beat down Missy?' to the list. There's a reason she's the Elder—*was* the Elder."

Mila smiled. "At least that one isn't too difficult to answer. You don't need to beat her down. I only need you to keep her busy while I deal with Azoth. Your job is to keep her from getting her hands on the device."

"Fair enough," Victoria conceded.

"I think I might have something to help with crowd control." Lance climbed off the couch and headed toward his and Rebecca's office. "Give me a second to grab the plans."

"The mines?" Rebecca called after him.

"Yeah, they might be perfect for this." He went around the corner, and they heard a door open then close.

"Okay, while we wait for Lance to return, any other ideas?" Mila opened the floor.

Remmy raised her hand.

The little goblin was wearing a pair of black shorts that

were so tight Mila suspected they were her boyshort underwear and had on a tie-dye cropped short-sleeve t-shirt that showed off her impressive abs and said, "Polo Fest 2016." She was sitting cross-legged on the floor in front of Danica, who leaned down from her club chair re-braiding Remmy's single long braid into multiple smaller ones that incorporated yellow and blue ribbons in the weave. She was then braiding the smaller braids into one another so that all of Remmy's hair ended up close to the scalp in a beautiful swirling design.

"What are you two doing? We're making a plan here, not having a slumber party." Mila suddenly felt annoyed for no good reason. She knew the two of them were paying attention regardless of what they happened to be doing. Mila rubbed her temple, her stomach suddenly feeling like it was regretting that second helping of pancakes. "I'm sorry. I didn't mean to snap. I think I'm overstressed and nervous. I know you're paying attention. Forgive me."

Danica smiled at Mila and continued to work her fingers expertly through Remmy's hair. "It's okay. You're doing great, babe. And this is an elven war braid. I'm always freaking out that someone will get their hand on Remmy's hair and pull her in during a battle. She uses speed and stealth to fight. Having to fight off an enemy while having her head pulled around would not end well for her." Danica focused on the braid work and smiled. "Plus, she'll look like a fucking badass."

Mila chuckled but had to agree that the braids had an air of badassery about them. She saw that Remmy still had her hand up, undeterred by Mila's outburst.

"Remmy, you don't have to raise your hand. What are you thinking?"

"You got it, boss lady. I was thinking that if the device works, but it's taking a long time, why not have the boss man drop Azoth into a pit and seal it up? That way no one can get to him and stop the process, but we can still focus on the fight."

Mila's brows came up in surprise. "That's a good idea. Would it be possible to do something like that?"

Finn pursed his lips for a second while he thought. "I don't think I can do a pit. The first time you and I fought him, I tried to spike him from below but couldn't affect the ground he was on. It was like he created a dead space in the earth. But, I could put him in a stone box—well, a pyramid would be faster, don't have to deal with the top of the box that way." He turned to Remmy and nodded approval. "Good thinking, Remmy. In fact, I think we should do it anyway, even if it's not taking too long. It would cut down on the one in a million shots."

"One in a million shots?" Victoria tucked her bare feet under herself on the couch.

"Yeah. For example, a thrall throws a rock at me and I dodge, but the rock happens to hit the device and knock it away from Azoth, cutting off the effect. Or someone stumbles into Azoth and knocks him away from the device. Over the years, I've learned that on a battlefield, one in a million happens about thirty percent of the time."

Victoria's brow screwed itself up as she looked at him. "You know that's not how statistics work, right?"

Finn harrumphed. "On the battlefield, statistics don't

mean shit. If it can go wrong, it will go wrong. Plan accordingly."

"I think it's a good idea to contain Azoth while the device does its thing. With one little difference. I need to be in there with him." She held up her hand, cutting off the multiple shouts of objection. "If we can't see him, then we won't know when it's time to strike. Me being in there makes this whole thing end that much quicker. Think of it this way. You won't have to watch my back."

"There is no way we can let you do that," Danica protested.

Victoria was close on her heels. "Agreed. What if we trap you in there with him and it doesn't work? He could gut you in an instant, or worse, devour you."

"I think it's a good idea." Finn shocked everyone. "Mila is powerful. If she sees it's not going the way it should, she can break herself out of the stone. She has plenty of strength to do that much. But if it's going to plan, then she can end it that much quicker while still cutting down on outside interference."

Mila felt a pride she didn't know was possible. Words like that from Finn were high praise. If he thought she would be fine, then she knew she would be.

Lance came back into the room with a device about the size of a hockey puck in his palm. It was made of black plastic-like material, with bronze-colored strips inlaid in an intricate pattern in the top that looked like a rune but with too many lines, like there were several runes laid atop one another.

"This is a prototype I put together. I figured it would be easier to see what it did than have me try to explain it." He placed the thing on the floor and pulled his wand from the pocket of his cargo shorts.

Mila saw that it was a hockey puck if the half-obscured NHL logo was any indication. Lance pointed his wand at it, and the brass-colored material absorbed the thin line of power that shot from the wand's tip.

"Here we go." He picked up his empty mug from the side table and tossed it over the puck.

A humming charge quickly built into a high-pitched tone before cutting off with a *whoosh!* A shimmering orb appeared above and touched the puck, making it look a little like a crystal ball. Floating in the center of the orb was the mug, hanging two feet off the ground.

No, Mila decided, floating wasn't the right word. The mug was stuck in the air. Like it had been wedged tight into the fabric of reality.

"This is a stasis mine." Finn stood and moved closer to it, slack-jawed wonder on his face. "Only the Imperial army has these. How they're built is one of the most tightly held secrets in the empire. How did you get one?"

"I made it in my office." Lance thumbed back over his shoulder toward the aforementioned room.

"You made this, just now?" Finn glanced down at the mine and shook his head in disbelief. "And you used a hockey puck?"

"It was the most mine-like thing I could find."

"You made one of the most advanced weapons in the universe out of spare parts in your office, and it took you about five minutes?" Finn repeated, to be absolutely clear.

"Yeah. Well, I did only make a small one. The inlay only

holds enough power for this small field, and even at this size—"

The field cut out and the mug hit the carpet with a soft *thump.*

"— it won't last long," he finished. "The full-sized ones will make a field forty feet across, but take quite a bit more power."

Finn turned to Mila and gave her a genuine smile. "We're going to be fine, babe."

"Okay, we have a start." Mila decided how to get things rolling. "Rebecca, Lance, and Finn, you three work on getting mines made. We need as many as you can get together by tonight. Victoria and I will look at the battlefield and get back to you with a solid target number for the mines. While we're doing that, we'll be charging the device as much as we can. Might as well get the most bang for the buck."

Mila turned to see that Danica was about three-quarters done with Remmy's hair. "Danica, can you and Remmy be our everything else? Watching Grimm, making food, and maybe give more great suggestions? I know we're going to miss things, and an extra pair of eyes or two will be helpful."

"We can do that." Danica paused her braiding and looked up at Mila. "Don't worry, Mila. We're going to be fine. Are you feeling okay? You look a little pale."

Mila let out a small acidic belch, hiding it behind a hastily raised fist. "I think I ate too many pancakes. I'll grab a water. It's fine."

"Okay, but if it keeps up, let me know."

Mila gave Danica a warm smile. "I will. Thanks, babe."

Victoria followed Mila to the dining table, where Lance had left a laptop for them to work on.

"What about Carl?" Victoria sat and opened the computer.

Mila sighed. She'd been going back and forth all morning if she should call the G.A.E.L. team in or not.

"Right now, I'm leaning toward leaving them out of it. With the mines working as a perimeter, we're going to be in pretty tight quarters. The last thing I want is to put people in danger when we don't need to. I was going to call them in if we didn't find a solution for crowd control, but with the mines I don't think we need them. This fight should only take a few minutes at most, and if it all goes according to plan, the only one who dies will be Azoth."

Victoria pulled up a program that used satellite imagery to show the entire surface of *Earth,* and started typing in coordinates. "What if it doesn't all go according to plan and we need to fight our way out? Or maybe the mines fail. Then we'll need the firepower. I can understand not wanting to put people in danger unnecessarily, but they're professionals and know how to handle themselves. I think we need them, if for nothing more than a little peace of mind."

Mila understood Victoria's concern and had to agree. But she still dreaded one of them getting hurt only to figure out that they didn't need to be there at all.

"You're probably right, but like you said, they're professionals. I'll call Carl tonight, explain the situation, and see what he thinks. The decision will be his."

Victoria nodded. "Probably the best course of action." She pointed at the screen as the globe in the app rotated.

"Here we go." The view dove into the atmosphere, and finally zoomed in on Iceland, then dove closer still. When the image stopped moving, it was near the center of the island nation in the middle of a flat field of black fine sand. Sharp pointed hills covered in green low-growing scrub surrounded the field like sleeping trolls. One side of the area butted up against a small, deep blue lake that looked cold even from a satellite.

It looked like the very definition of the middle of nowhere.

"Iceland? Why Iceland?"

"Because back then, it was the only large island not booked by any passengers. We needed to keep the fight away from prying eyes. No one was supposed to know there were any Valkyries on the ship, and a huge battle would have attracted notice. Luckily, it's still pretty empty." She glanced over at Mila. "You ready to figure this shit out?"

Mila drew a deep breath and shook her head. Pulling the device from the pocket of her dress, she held it up so Victoria could see it. "Let me put another charge in first."

Victoria groaned and stood. "Fine, but I'm making another pot of coffee."

By late afternoon, they'd picked their location and made the necessary measurements. Danica let the others know that they would need at least forty-five mines to get a perimeter large enough for them to move freely, but small enough that most of the enemy would portal in outside the safe zone.

The entire time, Mila and Victoria passed the device back and forth, charging it when their powers replenished themselves. By the time they were eating lunch it was obvious that Mila was charging the device two to one with Victoria, which had bothered the older Valkyrie, but also seemed to solidify some idea she had been thinking through about Mila.

At around four thirty Mila awoke with a start, as she felt herself falling out of her chair. She rubbed her eyes with the palms of her hands and looked over to see that Victoria wasn't doing any better. Charging the device continually felt like they had been lifting weights at the gym for seven hours straight.

"Come on." Mila tiredly climbed to her feet. "We need a nap. We're done charging that bottomless pit. If that's not enough power to kill that ugly fuck, then we're already doomed."

Victoria didn't answer, merely climbed out of her chair and stumbled toward her room.

Mila was only a few steps behind her.

CHAPTER TWENTY-TWO

"So, that's where we stand. The whole thing is going down tomorrow. I know it's short notice, but do you think you and the team can help me out one more time?" Mila spoke into the phone as she paced the deck beside the pool.

Thick clouds had rolled in during her nap. Now that the sun had set and the clouds were blocking the starlight, there weren't even the lowest light levels beyond the rails of the deck, only a never-ending darkness. Not that Mila was looking past the rails. There was something unsettling about looking into the pitch black that reminded her too much of Azoth.

"I think we can arrange something," Carl said on the other end of the line. "What did you have in mind?"

"Well, I hoped you might have some nonlethal options."

There was silence on the line for a second. "Nonlethal? Why?"

"I did say that there's potential to save many of the

attackers, right?" Now that she said it, she wasn't sure she had mentioned that fact to him in her summary.

"Oh, right. You mentioned that. Sorry. I was a little fixated on the main target." Carl laughed. "But yeah, we have nonlethal options. We can bring them both."

"Good, I was hoping you would say that." Mila didn't say more, thanks to a sudden urge to look out past the rails of the deck. It was like when you decided to watch a scary movie and you had to force yourself to watch, although your mind was telling you to look away. She shook herself and turned to look into the house. Everyone had gone to bed hours ago, but she had been putting off the call, instead going over plans she had gone over a thousand times.

"Hey, how's the construction at Preston's moving along? I hear he's putting in facilities to double the G.A.E.L. teams." Mila changed the topic as she saw that all the lights in the house were on, and wondered if she should turn them off when she went to bed, or if the house would take care of it.

"I have to ask you something." Carl sounded serious, and it snapped her wandering mind back to the present. "Why not give Azoth what he wants? Now, hear me out first. He tells you that if you bring the Reaper to him tomorrow, then he'll leave *Earth* alone. Bam, you saved the world. But if you don't, that's World War Three, this time with wizards. The choice seems pretty clear to me."

Mila laughed. "Are you serious? I give him the Reaper, and he and his people become the most powerful beings in the universe. They would destroy everything."

"True, but my job is to protect *Earth*, not the universe."

"I can't do that to those people, even if I never see them.

I would know that billions were dying every day because of the choice I made. And besides, who's to say he doesn't come back and destroy *Earth* anyway?"

"I hate to say this, but Azoth is unstoppable. If you kill him, he'll come back again. It's a never-ending cycle. The only way to truly get rid of him is to make him leave. Giving him the Reaper is the fastest way to do that. You would be a hero."

"I don't want to be a hero, Carl. I want to do the right thing for my people." She screwed up her face at that comment. Why had she called them *her* people? She shrugged. They were all Earthlings, she supposed. That kind of made them all the same people.

She heard him draw a calming breath. "You're going to start a war, child. Why do that? The answer is so easy. Give him the damned Reaper and be done with it."

"What's wrong with you? I'm not giving him the fucking Reaper, Carl. That's simply a longer form of suicide."

She was getting pissed. Who the fuck did he think he was? She thought he was a better person than someone who would sacrifice others to save his skin.

That itch at the back of her mind came again, this time stronger. She had an almost overwhelming desire to look out over the railing and try to spot something, anything out in the darkness. She didn't want to look out in the darkness, though, so instead she simply closed her eyes and crossed her arms as best she could while holding the phone to her ear.

"I'm sorry. I'm trying to understand your thinking here." Carl's voice was cooler now that he had a few seconds to think his words over. "Hey, where are you, anyway?"

"At a friend's. We were afraid that Missy might have figured out the condo's location, so we bugged out." At the phrase "bugged out," Mila suddenly realized how quiet it was out on the deck. Usually, there were at least half a million crickets and peepers singing their little horny hearts out.

"Are you still in Denver?" His tone was casual.

Why did he give a shit? "No, we left the state. Why do you want to know where I am?"

"No reason, simply making small talk. You're pretty lucky you left. A huge storm rolled in this afternoon—must have dumped an entire lake's worth of water on us in roughly half an hour. How's the weather where you are?" He sounded a little annoyed, which annoyed Mila right back.

"Look Carl, I like you, but you're starting to freak me out a little."

"Sorry. It's late," he said through a sudden yawn. "You woke me up when you called. I'm still trying to clear my head." There wasn't a hint of tiredness in his voice. "Okay, so if you won't give him the Reaper, then how do you plan on fighting him, little one? You must have some ace up your sleeve. Let me guess. It's the dwarf, isn't it?"

She swore she heard his eyes rolling with the question. And since when did Carl refer to Finn as "the dwarf"? Not to mention Carl had never called her "little one" before. That sounded like something...

Mila stopped pacing and listened to her surroundings. There wasn't anything. Not even the sound of the constant wind through the trees. No insects, no splashing turtles, or chirping frogs. Nothing.

Looking down at herself, she saw that she was wearing her leather pants and moto jacket, along with her corset and the gray V-neck t-shirt she had been wearing in San Francisco. She didn't remember changing out of the black skater dress. Hell, she didn't remember anything in any real detail beyond being on the phone with Carl.

Mila ground her teeth and growled low in her chest. This was all one of Azoth's constructs. Mila was still lying in bed in her black dress taking a nap, not pacing back and forth on the deck.

She considered going off on the asshole, really ripping into him, but she knew that would only make her feel slightly better. It would also be wasting an opportunity. She drew a deep breath and calmed herself.

"Are you still there?" Carl sounded suspicious.

"Yeah, I'm here. I was trying to figure out the best way to tell you the plan, but the truth is, we don't really have one. Right now, the best option we have is to lay a beat-down on that worm-footed failure. If we can beat him low enough, we might be able to kill him. I'll be honest with you, that's all we have."

"I don't know that you should talk that way about a being as powerful as Azoth." He forced a chuckle. "What if he heard you?" She heard the bristle in Carl's reply at the name-calling, but she pretended she didn't.

"Well, then I guess I would have to say it to his face. I mean, his void. I won't lie, I'm pretty sure that hole where his face should be goes so far back that it sucked up a big chunk of his brain." She really shouldn't be antagonizing him, but fuck it, the piece of shit deserved it. "I heard one of his thralls mumbling that Azoth smelled like he had shit himself, then took a bath in urine to clean himself off."

"That's impossible," Carl retorted with controlled anger. "Thralls can't speak of their own volition."

"Huh, maybe I was simply thinking it so hard I thought I heard the thrall say it. You know what? It doesn't matter. You've convinced me to bring the Reaper with me tomorrow. You're right, I don't know any of those people out there. If I can save *Earth*, that'll be enough for me. If the fight doesn't look like it's going my way, I'll give up and hand it over."

"Really?" Carl sounded both surprised and overjoyed at the same time. It was some of the worst acting Mila had ever heard. "You're making the right decision."

"I suppose I am." She almost left it at that, but couldn't help getting one last dig in on the cocky idiot. "You know what I always wondered?"

"No, what do you wonder, child?"

"Well, it's a given that he uses those disgusting tentacles to pleasure himself." She waited for the reaction.

There was a lengthy pause, then a confused, "What?"

"But the part I always wondered about is how many he uses at once."

"What? How da—"

"I'm willing to bet it's twelve," she added matter-of-factly, then waited. She knew he would need to know why she thought it was specifically that number. She only needed to wait.

After almost fifteen long seconds of Carl's voice

making strangled growls, he finally asked, "Why do you think it's twelve?"

"Because his head looks like it's about as big as eleven tentacles mashed together, and he has his head shoved up his ass so often that he would need to add the extra tentacle to feel anything."

Mila almost laughed at the sound of angry breathing coming through the line, but she knew he would play it out since she'd told him her "plans." If he outed himself now, then she would change them. It was childish, but she hated him enough to do it anyway.

"Isn't that funny, Carl?" she goaded.

For a second, she thought she might have gone one step too far, but eventually he answered. "That's quite humorous, child. Very funny indeed. Perhaps I shall pull a joke on you in Iceland tomorrow, to show you how funny I thought it was." His voice was practically a speak-and-spell, he was so monotone.

"Okay, see you there, buddy." She mustered all the enthusiasm she could.

He hung up.

Mila stared daggers at the phone, then threw it out into the darkness as far as she could, letting a scream of rage chase after it. She didn't want the phone anywhere near her after being forced to talk to that slimy asshole through it.

When she finally heard it splash into the swampy waters far below, she took off at the rail in a full-on sprint, and launched herself into the darkness.

Sucking in a deep breath, Mila sat up in the guest room bed, her eyes wide and heart pounding. She took a few seconds to calm herself before looking down and confirming she was once again wearing her black skater dress. She flexed her toes, admiring the black lacquer toenail polish as it glinted in the light.

Knowing you're out of a dream is all about the details. Turns out that brains are lazy, and if you look too closely at anything in a dream for too long, it never looks quite right.

Ever since she realized that little fact, Mila had made a point of painting a small rune on each of her big toenails before applying her customary black polish. Doing so left the paint over the rune ever so slightly thicker, and if she wiggled her toes in the light she could make out the runes' outline. It was her surefire way of knowing she was truly awake.

Finn had painted the runes the first couple of times until Mila could do it herself. When he asked what she wanted them to say she'd told him it should say whatever he wanted to tell Azoth.

It turned out that writing "fuck" and "off" in Dwarvish was super easy.

CHAPTER TWENTY-THREE

As she padded out into the kitchen, Mila heard talking and bubbling water coming from outside. She checked the clock on the wall and saw that it was only a little past nine. While it was later than she would have liked, it was still early evening for her and Finn, especially when you factored in the time change.

Walking out onto the deck, she spied Danica, Finn, Lance, and Rebecca all sitting in the hot tub, enjoying a drink after the long day they had put in.

Danica was the first to spot Mila and waved before shouting over the sound of the bubbles. "The suits are in my room. Go grab one and come join us."

Mila waved and decided a hot soak might do her some good after her encounter with Azoth. She went to Danica's room and found the suits laid out as though Danica had looked at each one before choosing the perfect one for the night. Mila laughed while thinking of her friend putting effort into something so dumb as picking a swimsuit to soak in a hot tub with friends.

Mila grabbed the first suit she saw, the same blue-and-white striped one Danica had worn the day before, and pulled the dress over her head. She hung the dress in the closet and stripped the rest of the way, tossing her underthings in the hamper.

Lifting the top to her chest, Mila caught another suit laid out on the far side of the bed. It was the black and orange one she had worn with Finn the first time they had used a hot tub together. She tossed the blue-and-white striped top back on the bed and walked over to the black and orange one.

As she was reaching for the second suit, she suddenly had the most stupid crisis of conscience in her life. She had mentally berated her friend for doing what she was doing right now. And it made her feel bad enough that she considered going back to her original choice out of guilt for abandoning it.

She stopped herself after a step and sighed dramatically. "This is so stupid. What are you doing? Put on the black and orange one, Mila. You want to wear that one. It has sentimental value, and your ass looks amazing in it. Quit fucking around and get moving."

She stood in shocked silence at her outburst for a good twenty seconds before she put on the black and orange one and headed out of the room.

As she passed the discarded blue and white bikini, she mumbled, "Sorry," for reasons beyond her understanding.

Right before she stepped out into the hall, she spotted the duffel bag she had packed all their clothes in on the built-in dresser. She saw something glinting from inside the open zipper and walked over to fish out whatever it was.

She pulled the glass cube Yaminah had given her out of the bag and stared at it for a few seconds before taking it with her back to the hot tub.

"It's my favorite suit!" Finn yelled when Mila stepped out onto the deck and headed their way.

Mila turned a little red at the attention, but also smiled like a schoolgirl. It was the exact reaction she wanted from him when she went with this suit over the other, which should have justified her choice, but she still felt a tiny bit of guilt about the whole thing.

She was slightly disappointed that the tub wasn't hotter when she slipped into the tub between Rebecca and Finn, but Mila figured that with a young kid, they probably kept it cooler for him.

"Hot enough for you?" Lance asked, his face flushed red from the heat.

Rebecca and Danica were flushed as well, but Finn looked cool as a cucumber.

"Yup, it's fine. I don't want to be the cause of anyone's heatstroke, though. You can turn it down if you want."

Finn chuckled, put his arm around her, and pulled her close. "I told them it wouldn't make a difference to me if they turned it up or not, but they cranked it up anyway."

"Have you guys ever felt guilty for choosing an article of clothing then deciding on something else and putting the first one back?" Mila asked, her guilt still bothering her.

Finn and Lance both laughed out loud, but Danica was looking at Mila with a raised eyebrow and Rebecca smiled at some fond memory.

"I take that as a no?" Mila asked, looking at each of them in turn.

When she got to Rebecca, she saw the woman nodding. "Oh yeah, I used to do stuff like that to myself all the time when I was pregnant with Grimm. I remember one time when Lance came into the laundry room to find me curled up in a ball crying my eyes out—I'm talking snot bubbles kind of crying. When he asked me what was wrong, he was shaking with fear that I had done something horrible, or something horrible had happened to me or the baby. It took him four hours to stop laughing when I told him I was crying because there were an odd number of socks, which meant that one sock was out there all alone and afraid that we abandoned it."

"Holy shit, it wasn't anything that bad." Mila laughed, her mood rising exponentially.

"You want a drink? We brought out some mixers or beers if you're feeling plebe," Lance offered, holding up his cheap domestic beer.

"As your doctor, I recommend that you only have one drink, or stick with water. You're stressed to hell, and I know you don't drink enough water every day. The way you've been burning through magic loading that device up, I'm surprised you can form coherent sentences," Danica cut in while giving her a motherly stare.

Mila laughed. "Okay mom, but only because you're my doctor, too. Actually, a sparkling water sounds pretty good. Danica's right, I don't drink enough water as it is, but add on the stress of the last couple of days, and it explains a lot."

Lance pulled a can of flavored sparkling water from a

small fridge that wasn't there a second ago and handed it to her.

Mila set the glass cube on the edge of the hot tub so she could open the can.

"What's this?" Rebecca picked up the cube and inspected it.

"It's the spying device Yaminah gave me. I was going to use it, but I'm afraid it's a trap. We can't decide if Yaminah is on the up-and-up or not."

"I can tell you if it's legit or not," Lance offered. He reached behind himself to a coat rack that normally stood in the hallway and pulled a wand from the pocket of a bathrobe hanging there.

He took the cube and held it close to his face while flicking his wand in a particular pattern as the tip glowed faintly. After half a minute or so, he handed the cube back to Mila and tossed his wand over his shoulder. It never hit the deck. Instead, it simply wasn't there anymore.

"It's clean. It only receives information, and the way it's made won't allow it to send anything. Whoever made it knew what they were doing."

"That's it? That was all it took?" Mila was shocked by how easy that was.

"Pretty much."

"The part you didn't see," Rebecca gave Lance a look that said they'd had this conversation before, "was the twenty years of intense study that came before. Stop being so modest, babe. You're an amazing witch."

Lance turned a little redder, if that was possible, but nodded. "She's right. That was a badass spell. But it doesn't change the fact that you can use the cube with no fear of being tracked."

"You should power it up," Rebecca suggested.

"She's right," Finn chimed in. "We might get a glimpse of what he's bringing to the table. Could help us with last-minute strategies."

"Are we all good with this?" Mila looked for any shaking heads, but saw only shrugs and nods. "Okay then, let's see what the rat bastard is up to."

Mila gripped the cube in one palm and fed a trickle of power into it. As soon as she did, golden light swirled at the cube's center. The next thing they knew, a sphere with a real-time, 360-degree feed from right above Azoth's hood surrounded them.

What they saw sobered them all.

Wherever the Drude was it was already late morning or early afternoon, with the sun high in a cloudless blue sky. He stood on a short grassy hill, his arms raised above his head as he chanted in a language that Mila had never heard before.

Missy was beside and slightly behind Azoth. Her cuts from the fight with Penny healed. Even the scarring was gone by this point although the empty charred eye socket remained, the dragon's fire rendering healing potions next to useless.

On his other side and much further back was Yaminah's robed figure. She was playing the meek and defeated slave, but the occasional look of pure hatred directed at the back of Azoth's hood told a different story altogether.

But the thing that had them speechless wasn't the faces of their well-known enemies, it was the endless sea of new faces fanned out before Azoth's spread arms. As he chanted, waves of black and purple miasma rolled from his fingers and flowed over the mass of people. With each wave, the crowd swayed like prairie grass in a light breeze.

Mila tried to spot the end of the sea of people, but they sort of blended in with the green and brown plains after a while.

"That's a lot more than a hundred and fifty thousand people." Finn scanned the image. "I would guess twice that, maybe two-and-a-half times." He put a gentle hand on Mila's shoulder and pointed to the front of the crowd. "I don't know if you noticed yet, but I don't think you need to call Carl anymore. He'll already be there."

Mila looked where he was pointing and gasped. Carl was dead center in the miasma wave, still wearing his tactical gear and holding his rifle. Quickly scanning the front ranks, Mila picked out Nick, Tina, Howard, and Jenny along with at least three other full teams of G.A.E.L. troopers. Every last one of them was well and truly under Azoth's spell.

CHAPTER TWENTY-FOUR

Mila dropped the cube to the deck as she stepped out of the water, not even noticing the chill anymore. The large viewing sphere flickered then died as the magic she'd supplied ran out.

What was she doing? There were people out there who needed her, and she was sitting around in a hot tub like an asshole. Her fists clenched at her sides as she walked toward the kitchen, water dripping from her in spattering trails.

She stopped before walking in, realizing she would drip all the way through the house, and looked around for a towel, but the closest thing she saw was a throw blanket over the back of a cushioned lounger beside the fire pit.

Mila clenched her teeth as she growled and turned to go back toward the tub, and the pile of towels Lance had brought and left on a lounge chair for them. She felt like a caged dog, all aggression and pent-up energy but no way to let it out. Even in sleep she couldn't get the satisfaction of peaceful rest. Her body was changing faster than she could keep up with, and in ways she couldn't predict.

Was she a Valkyrie, a dwarf, a Peabrain, or something else entirely? What was more frustrating was that no one had any real answers for her, only speculation and hypothesis, half of which made it sound like she should stop shaving her legs and start wearing patchouli oil in her hair.

She wasn't looking where she was going anymore, only walking fast to get there, so when Finn wrapped her up in a towel from behind and pulled close in his big arms, she almost punched him in pure reaction.

She was shaking, her mind going a thousand miles an hour, but with nowhere to go she was only spinning her tires.

"You're spiraling, darlin,'" Finn murmured in her ear as he held her back to his chest, his arms around her holding the towel closed.

"I know I am, and it's driving me insane. Fucking Azoth never relents. He's like an annoying bully that picks and picks until you're ready to explode, but when you finally swing, you find out that he's also bigger and stronger than you. And one of the worst parts is, the one friend you have that could come up with a half-decent plan to win the fight is in a coma-like sleep wrapped around her eggs, which makes my heart forget to beat sometimes thinking about having babies in the house. How are we going to protect them from assholes in the future? Not to mention I'm pretty sure I'm pregnant now, because I felt guilty about not wearing a fucking bathing suit." She pressed her lips together as she grabbed the edge of the towel and wiped the water from her face. She felt like she needed to be doing something, but she didn't know what that was.

"I know you're upset, and feel like you need to be out there doing something. I feel that too." Finn spoke in his maddeningly calm tone. It sometimes felt like a designer drug created to calm Mila down. "But we prepared what we could already. There's a stack of fifty mines we made today, ready to go and charged up. You've put all the magic you and Victoria could into the device. If it doesn't have enough charge by now, then it never will. We all know our part to play in the battle. Now is the hardest part."

"The waiting." She sighed, her nerves a few degrees less frazzled than they had been a few minutes ago.

"No, the waiting is time passing by. The hardest part is relaxing. You can't go into battle a bundle of raw nerves. That's a good way to get yourself killed." As he talked, he slowly led her toward an oversized plush lounging chair Mila was pretty sure wasn't there a few minutes ago. "You've had friends and allies with you every time you've faced Azoth, but you keep trying to fight him all on your own. This is our fight, not your fight." He stopped beside the lounger and turned her in his arms so he was looking down into her eyes, their faces only inches apart. "You're the strongest person I've ever met, Mila. Stronger than a dwarf, a Valkyrie, or a human—you're all of those things at once, but that's not why you're so strong."

She smiled up at him and his goofy over-the-top praise, but she couldn't help feeling like he meant every word. "Oh? So why am I so strong, my great and wise dwark?"

He smiled, his white teeth shining through his thick brown beard, and a glint in his eye that let her know he was about to hit her with the sincerest cheesy line she was likely to ever hear in her life. Her cheeks already hurt from the grin plastered on her face, and he hadn't said anything yet.

"Because you give a shit."

Mila snorted a laugh. "What?"

"Do you have any idea how many people out there in the wide universe truly give a shit about others?"

"Lots of people give a shit, Finn. It's called compassion. Most people have it in spades," she argued.

He shook his head slightly. "I'm not talking about compassion. I'm talking about picking up a stranger and his dragon friend at a gas station in the middle of the night because you understood that they needed your help. I'm talking about wrestling hellhounds to the ground with your bare hands to save strangers in a bar. How about grabbing a woman bent on killing you and taking the time to fix her while standing in the middle of a war zone? Or barricading yourself in a bar and fighting off dozens of eight-foot-tall wolfmen to give people time to escape? Do I need to continue?"

Mila shook her head. "I get it. I'm willing to sacrifice myself for others."

He laughed and shook his head. "No, dummy. You're *not* willing to sacrifice yourself. If you were, then you would give Azoth the Reaper, or have killed that woman instead of fixing her, or left me at the Kum & Go—and you would've killed a little piece of your soul each time you did until there was nothing left. You're strong because you're willing to be scared out of your mind, or chased by evil witches for months, or have to fight off roving hit squads, as long as you're doing the right thing."

Mila swallowed, finally starting to get what he was saying.

"You're spiraling over this battle because you can't figure out what the right choice is. This is the classic ruler's dilemma. You know what to do to have the best outcome, but your chances of accomplishing that best outcome are problematic. The real dilemma, however, comes when weighing the consequences. If you succeed, it saves your people. If you fail, then your people are dead and the enemy gets what they want anyway. But if you give in and give the enemy what they want, then your people are safe but others will suffer. This one is so hard to wrap your head around because the battle isn't about your people, it's about everyone else. Two out of those three choices mean your people are safe, but two out of those three choices end with everyone else dead or suffering. The only way to save them both is the largest gamble, with the highest consequences for failure."

Mila felt her anxiety rise as he laid it all out for her. The magnitude of her choices was overwhelming. All she could think about was, what if she lost? That was the only option where everyone died, her people and everyone else.

Her heart rate shot up, and she must have gotten a panicked look in her eye because Finn spoke faster, trying to get to the point quickly.

"This is good news for someone like you, darlin'. You only have one choice. You can't sacrifice yourself for the half win, and losing is never the option against an evil like Azoth. Your only option is to fight and win. You can let go of the choices. They don't matter to you. Logically, you want the easy way—give him what he wants and we're all safe—but you can't do that because the easy way is for cowards, and you are not a coward.

"Let it all go. The choice was made the second you found out Azoth existed. It was always going to come down to this battle in a few hours. So, relax. Take some time to recover before the battle. Clear your mind of doubt so you can focus on what needs to happen. Then, when the time comes, we go to Iceland and do whatever it takes to win. If we have to make the entire island uninhabitable for the next thousand years, it will be worth it. Whatever it takes."

"Whatever it takes," she echoed, feeling the confusion and pressure fall away, leaving her feeling light and free.

He pushed her, and she let out a squeal as she lost her balance and fell into the cushioned lounge chair.

Finn straddled the end of the lounger and took her left foot in both of his large hands, massaged the stress from her with his thumbs.

Her eyes rolled back and she collapsed into the lounger. "Oh, fuck. I needed that."

"So, you think you're pregnant?" His voice was entirely too casual.

"Not really." Mila laughed, then pursed her lips in thought. "Well, it has crossed my mind, but I don't think so." He nodded and focused on the foot rub. After half a minute, she couldn't hold it in any longer. "Five percent chance."

Finn lifted a brow, but didn't look up from her foot. "One in twenty? Really?"

"Ten percent."

"How about we ask Danica to do a test after this is all over? Your statistics are all over the place, and I'm not a hundred percent sure you know how they work." He glanced up at her and cracked a smile. "See, that's the proper way to use them. Make it sound precise while not really making a statement."

"I am a hundred percent sure you're a dork."

"I'm a hundred percent sure that you like that about me."

Mila rolled her eyes and laughed.

CHAPTER TWENTY-FIVE

Mila finally relaxed with the help of Finn and his magic thumbs. They went back to the hot tub and laughed and talked about the future with friends. Remmy and Victoria eventually came out to join them and they made a little food and shared a last meal before it was time to get ready.

Finn double-checked that Mila had her two healing potions and that her weapons were secure in her corset holster while Mila went over how to activate the device once again. She worried that she would mess up the sequence, so she had been drilling it into her muscle memory every time she filled. She could now do the sequence by feel alone.

Once fully dressed and kitted out, they looked into one another's eyes, enjoying a last quiet moment.

"Ready?" Finn asked.

Mila nodded and pulled him down for a kiss.

That done, she picked up the Reaper's case and pulled

the shoulder strap over her chest, securing the black case to it.

They walked down the hall and stopped at Penny's chamber to check on her before they left. She was still in the same position, feeding her eggs a steady diet of magic while she dreamed.

Mila blew the sleeping dragon a kiss. "See you soon, Penny."

They headed out to the deck and discovered that they were the last ones there.

Remmy was in her leathers, her hair up in the intricate braids Danica had done for her and her daggers strapped across the small of her back. Victoria wore a pair of jeans and a gray long-sleeved t-shirt with her longsword strapped to her back, the pommel sticking up over her shoulder. Danica had gone for black leggings and a matching black compression shirt, keeping her clothing tight so it wouldn't interfere with her bow.

Everyone had a determined look on their face and stood tall, ready to face what came.

Rebecca came out, struggling to carry a large duffel bag. Finn quickly stepped forward and took it from her.

"Thanks." She brushed off the lap of her white leggings and matching compression shirt. She looked like Danica, but in reverse. Mila saw that she had strapped a thin white sheath to each thigh and the handles of three wands poked out of each.

"What are you doing?" Mila asked when it became clear Rebecca wasn't coming over to say goodbye.

"Lance and I drew straws, and I'm the one who gets to go with you," she answered matter-of-factly.

"You're doing nothing of the sort. You have Grimm. I can't let you go out there and risk not coming home," Mila argued.

"Because I have a child does not mean that I sit by when my friends are in need."

"I understand that, but there's no need. We have a plan, and you don't have to get in the line of fire to accomplish it. You're not coming."

Rebecca drew a deep breath. "You can't stop me from helping you. Lance and I made our choice, and I was chosen. This is as much our fight as it is yours."

Mila opened her mouth to retort but Finn beat her to it, his voice commanding and firm but still kind. "Rebecca, we have our plan to defeat Azoth. You're part of it, but, your role isn't on the front line. We need you here. You're the last line of defense if this all goes to shit. We'll need you to let the world know what's happening. More importantly, though, I need you to watch over Penny. She is one of the few faerie dragons left, and right now she's more vulnerable than she's ever been. I promised her I would watch over her when she laid her eggs. I need you to stand that guard for me. Can you do that?"

Rebecca swallowed, obviously affected by the words, but to Mila it seemed like she was a little too affected by them. Mila would have sworn that Rebecca was fighting to not bow as she backed away.

"I can do that. Sorry. I hadn't realized how important it was for me to stay. We'll see you when you get back. Penny will be safe in our care, I promise."

Mila raised an eyebrow at Finn, who shrugged. "Everyone ready?"

There were nods all around and they gathered in close. Danica fed her spell, then they disappeared with a light popping sound.

As soon as they left, whatever Finn had done to Rebecca lifted and she shook her head in confusion. Then her face narrowed as she stared through the spot they'd departed from.

"You conniving dwarf. That's the last time your royal mantle works on me." She was half-pissed and half-impressed, but ultimately she saw the point of him telling her to stay. Either that, or his mantle of authority was far subtler than she thought.

She narrowed her eyes and looked over her shoulder at Lance standing in the kitchen with a big grin on his face. He had said Finn would make her stay, but she didn't think he would be so powerful.

Good thing they were friends. She would hate to see how he handled his enemies.

The first thing Mila noticed about Iceland was how wet it was. While it wasn't currently raining where they stood, she saw a cloud dumping a hefty shower across the sand fields less than half a mile away. The air was thick with moisture in a completely different way than at Rebecca's house in the bayou. While the swamp was sticky wet, on the sand fields it was more of a lubricating feel.

The second thing Mila noticed was the location's eerie beauty. It truly was like no other place on *Earth*. Fine black sand stretched as far as the eye could see, broken only by miniature mountains covered in vibrant green moss, or maybe they were full-sized mountains covered in grass—Mila couldn't find a familiar reference to tell the difference. There were no trees. There were no animals. It was only endless black sands, mountains, and a lake that was either massive and surrounded by mountains, or was fairly small and surrounded by hundred-foot-tall pointy hills. The entire place made her feel off-balance in some unexplainable way.

"How does a place like this happen? And then to have it only happen once across the entire planet?" Mila slowly spun in a circle while taking in the oddly mesmerizing view.

"It was a custom berth." Victoria squinted into the sudden daylight after the near pitch-black of the bayou, although thick cloud cover tempered the sun.

The statement was a sharp reminder to Mila that *Earth* was in fact a ship. She knew it was, but she freely admitted that she didn't *understand* it.

"I thought you said it was one of the few empty places to have the first battle with Azoth. If someone had this made…"

Finn looked around at what they had to work with, then set the duffel on the ground and unzipped it, revealing stacks of heavily modified hockey pucks.

"It was empty," Victoria continued the story as she took the half-dozen mines Finn handed her, "but only because when the Huldu found out what she intended to transport, they freaked the fuck out. They even gave her a full refund, which is insane, if you know any Huldu."

Finn passed out a stack to each of them, then pointed to

five places in a circle around them and assigned each of them a spot. "Once you're in the general area, I can better direct you where to place them. Set them on the ground and I'll bury them all at once."

They all headed to their assigned places, and Finn had them place their first mine then walk to the right about fifteen steps and place the next, adjusting as necessary. When they ran out of mines, they came back to the duffel and restocked. They had the mines placed to Finn's satisfaction in less than twenty minutes.

Mila and the others stood to one side, watching as Finn dropped to a knee and placed his palm on the ground. After a second, purple energy shot from his hand into the black sand.

The sound of a huge drum being struck a single blow rang out from below. The percussive note made the top three inches of sand in a half-mile radius leap a couple of feet into the air. Since the sand was fairly damp there was no dust cloud, and when it had all settled back to the ground, it was the same color as the surrounding sand.

The effect was twofold. First, it buried all the mines under an inch or two of sand, making them invisible to the enemy, and second, it erased all their footprints from setting the mines. Now it looked like they had just arrived and only moved around in the immediate area.

"What about the bag?" Danica pointed at the empty duffel.

"Uh," Finn looked around for somewhere to stash it, but there was nothing that would hide the large bag. He dropped to a knee and dug a hole with his hands, then folded the bag into a flat square and laid it in the hole before shoveling the sand back over it. Then he stood and stomped the loose sand down. "There. It's gone."

"That works." Danica leaned on her bow and clicked her tongue a few times out of boredom. "What time are we supposed to meet up with hole in the face?"

"The original battle happened just after six in the morning." Victoria checked her watch. "Which is in roughly ten minutes. Maybe we should look and see what he's up to?"

Mila pulled the cube out of her pocket and channeled magic into it. While it gathered speed in the center of the cube, Mila turned to Victoria. "What was the animal or whatever that the person wanted to bring here?"

Victoria shuddered. "Bunnycorn."

Mila laughed. "Bunnycorn? Like a bunny with a horn on its forehead?"

"Exactly. Disgustingly dangerous things. More than one empire has tried to exterminate them from the universe, but they all fail."

"A bunnycorn? Why would you need a place like this to —"the cube coming to life cut off her question.

They saw a dark room with a single light hanging from the ceiling over Azoth's head. Missy stood beside him, and Yaminah was a few steps behind. They waited in silence for some unseen cue.

Mila noticed Yaminah glance up at where the cube's view originated and give a slight nod.

Mila had decided that she would use any help Yaminah could provide, but she wasn't counting on it for anything. It looked like she would keep her word.

At some unseen prompt, Missy raised her hand and created a void portal. The same portal ripped open through the translucent edge of the viewing sphere.

Mila killed the magic to the cube and shoved it in her pocket as Missy stepped through the opening. She gave them all a one-eyed, hate-filled look before stepping to the side.

Azoth came through, his tentacles slithering him across the sands in an even speed that left his torso unmoving and creating the impression that he was floating.

The hood swiveled and he took in the group arrayed before him, but focused on Mila when he spoke.

"You have brought quite a few allies for a simple hand-off, child." While his voice was full of grinding screeching sounds, his sarcasm was still evident. "Perhaps I should bring a few friends of mine?"

A few dozen portals ripped open in a circle around them. Then more portals opened behind those. And more beyond those. Within seconds, there were thousands of portals spaced out over the entire sand field.

"Why don't you say hello to a few of my closest friends?" Azoth's smugness made Mila feel like she needed a shower.

Mila left the portals to her team. She only had Azoth to deal with.

She locked her eyes on the tall Drude, narrowed them, and put her hands in her jacket pockets. Then Mila took the device in her left hand and began the short but complicated series of touchpoints to activate it. At each finger press, she left a small pool of magic as the device tried to suck it from her fingers.

"Hey, fuckface." Mila stepped close to the towering creature. "Do you like apples?

CHAPTER TWENTY-SIX

Penny knew she was asleep. At least, it was something like sleep. She was aware of some things, but others seemed like they were on the other side of the universe.

She knew someone had teleported her to Rebecca's and Lance's, along with her hoard and eggs, but she had no idea who had done it. She could sometimes hear voices of people talking to her, but she didn't understand the words, as if they had all started speaking a new language while she was sleeping.

The only thing Penny was fully aware of was the sky-blue void she inhabited while in her coma-like state. She didn't have a body in the void, but that didn't matter to her. The void was for things beyond her body.

Spiraling out from the never-ending blue nothing were tendrils of her person. Not the physical parts, but the parts that made up who she was as a person. Each of the tendrils reached out to connect to one of her trusted family members.

She had collected her family with care, although most

would say she had left it up to luck. The only member of her family that she had actively sought out was Finn. The moment she had met him, she knew he was exactly what she was looking for. Unwavering, confident, and sure of who he was and his place in the universe, Finn was the ideal person to connect her to the outside world away from her kind.

Penny differed from most dragons. Dragons as a race are micro-managers—they want control of every aspect of whatever they're doing. But Penny quickly realized that if she wanted to get ahead, she had two choices—learn how to do everything on her own, or find people that could do those things better than her while she focused on what she was good at.

That's where Finn came in. She found him because she knew he would never settle for anyone less than ideal for himself. A person who was ideal for him would be a perfect member of her family.

It took far longer than she thought it would, but sure enough, he found Mila, and through Mila, Danica.

The three of them covered all the ground she needed to finally give birth to her eggs.

And now, she watched as the tendrils reached out to the three of them, feeding them the part of her that she viewed as most important to raising her children.

Faerie dragons were unlike all other dragons in that they were small and vulnerable if caught sleeping. Her kind evolved to sleep less than others to mitigate danger and learned to convert food into magic so they could use it to power spells while they were unconscious. They evolved in a million little ways, but the one that set them apart the most was how they incubated their eggs.

Inevitably, they had to lay there for a time, feeding their eggs. During this time, they were more vulnerable than at any other point in their lives. Not only were they forced to sleep for long periods, but their magic was solely devoted to enriching and growing their babies, so they had nothing left for defense. Early on, many young faerie dragons were killed before their eggs could hatch, leading to a sharp decline in their numbers they never recovered from.

As a solution, they gathered treasure that had to contain the hopes and dreams of those who tried to own it. Those feelings of hope and freedom became infused in the treasure itself, and the faerie dragons used it as power to supplement their limited magical stores. It also served a second purpose as an emergency magical fund that would allow the eggs to mature over time, even if the parent were to die halfway through the process.

If a parent happened to not be there when their babies hatched, then the babies became nothing more than wild animals. To solve this, the parent connected themselves to the eggs with one of those tendrils of self—intelligence. Upon their death, that intelligence would transfer to the child, allowing them to retain sentience without imprinting.

But that left the problem of baby dragons without parents, which was where the tendrils leading to Finn, Danica, and Mila came in. Penny had come to know and love them and knew beyond a shadow of a doubt that they would raise her children as theirs if need be. So Penny had selected the three things she viewed as most important for a dragon to be raised properly.

To Finn, she connected her protective self, the part of her that would kill without hesitation to save her children.

To Danica, she connected her love and forgiveness and penitence, which turned out to be all the same thing to one degree or another.

She gave the hardest one to Mila by connecting her motherhood to the Valkyrie. Mila would become her children's guiding light if Penny were to die during the process. This had other complications, like feeling all the things Penny had felt as her body grew the eggs inside her. She would be moody and more than likely feel ill occasionally, but it was the most important of the tendrils, and she wanted Mila to be their mother if she could not.

She hoped Mila would understand when she explained it later. It was a great honor.

Penny became aware of her magic running dry. She would soon wake to feed before coming back. Sometimes, Penny wished she could channel magic like Peabrains. The thought of unlimited power was tempting, but that part where they had a max flow was the real kicker. If she needed to use everything she had in one massive go, she could. There was power in the ability to be reckless.

A thought occurred to her that seemed strange and out of place at first, but then she caught a memory of Mila talking to her about the device. Something about finding flaws in it.

Not having anything else to do but wait for her magic to drain enough that she woke up to feed, Penny started going over the plans for the device. She had studied each part when they were building it, and at the time it looked perfectly capable of doing what Gregory had said it should, but Penny's thought about the limited flow of Peabrain magic was sticking in her head.

She went over the parts again, putting the device together in her blue void. On the third time reassembling the device, she caught what was bothering her. The passage the magic flowed through was large compared to the flow that a witch or a Peabrain would need, but for someone like Penny or Mila, who could expend enormous amounts of power at the drop of a hat, it was rather limiting.

In fact, it was so limiting that Penny was more than sure that a Drude at full strength could easily convert the flow coming out of the device to infernal magic . The device would become less of a weapon *against* a Drude, and more like a battery *for* it.

Penny considered a few design changes and was sure she could fix the problem. It would be a shame, because Mila and Victoria would have to start over with the charging process, although with her new design they could cut their charging time to seconds, not minutes.

Penny felt her magic finally run dry, and she was pulled out of her subconscious and groggily shoved back into the waking world.

Yawning and stretching, Penny's last thought before hopping off the hoard and heading for the kitchen was, "It's a good thing Mila doesn't plan to use the device any time soon."

Rebecca was trying not to bite her nails while she sat at the dining table and stared out at the deck, waiting for her friends to return. Her leg couldn't stop bouncing with nervous energy and while her leg distracted her, she started biting her thumbnail.

Something blue and about the size of a cat jumped up on the table right beside her, making her scream bloody murder and fall out of the chair. In the blink of an eye, she was back on her feet with a wand in each hand pointed at Penny.

Rebecca let out the breath she'd been holding and holstered her wands in the thigh sheaths. "You scared the bejesus out of me! What are you doing up? Don't you have to incubate your eggs?"

In answer, Penny tiredly pointed at her open mouth with a talon.

Understanding immediately, Rebecca grabbed a banana from the fruit bowl on the island and handed it to Penny who nodded and sat on her haunches, peeled the banana and had half of it gone before Rebecca could open the fridge to find a high-calorie snack for Penny while the witch made her a proper meal. She pulled out a plate of cold shrimp scampi from the other night and held it up for Penny to see.

"How about shrimp?"

Penny nodded while swallowing the last of the banana and reaching for the plate.

"I can heat them up if you want."

Penny gave her a deadpan look, then puffed a flame from her nostril.

"Oh, right." Rebecca came back to the table, set the plate in front of Penny, and retook her seat.

Penny munched on shrimp and became more with it with each tail she piled on the table. She finally took a break from stuffing her face and spoke, making Rebecca snap out of her worried haze. "Shir?"

Rebecca gave her a "what are you talking about" look. "What do you mean, where is everyone? They're facing off with Azoth."

The next shrimp stopped halfway to Penny's mouth. "Chi?"

"Yeah, with the device. How else are they supposed to do it?"

The shrimp fell to the table as Penny charged forward. The little dragon grabbed two handfuls of Rebecca's shirt and shook her with everything she had. One long jet of flame shot from her left nostril, accompanied by a wild-eyed look.

"Wait a minute! You're telling me that not only will the device not work on a Drude, it'll make him stronger?" Rebecca went white with fear before pulling out one of her wands and forming a teleport bubble.

CHAPTER TWENTY-SEVEN

Mila hit the last spot on the device and felt it hum with power. Dumping as much of her magic into her body as she dared, Mila increased her strength, speed, and endurance to superhuman levels.

As fast as she could, Mila stepped close to Azoth and withdrew the brass ball of vibrating power from her pocket, then slammed it into the void he called a face.

"How do you like them apples?" she shouted while dancing back and pulling Gram with one hand and the Ivar with the other.

Azoth's hands went to the opening of his hood as he screamed and stumbled back.

Taking quick aim, Mila blasted the shocked Missy in the chest with the pistol as she whispered Gram's power word, followed by the word for her chainmail armor. The sword folded open, and the armor flowed up out of her skin, covering her torso in cool fine-mesh Mythril.

The Ivar bolt caught Missy flatfooted and exploded

against her collarbone. She tumbled backward across the black sand.

The area clear, Mila turned to Azoth and stepped close. "Do it, Finn!"

No sooner had the words left her mouth when four giant triangular slabs of dark gray stone shot out of the ground at a forty-five-degree angle, quickly covering Mila and Azoth in a stone pyramid that cut off the sun and the sounds of thousands charging out of void portals.

Azoth was still screaming, tearing at his hood, and backpedaling in an erratic panicked shuffle of tentacles. It took a second for Mila's dark vision to kick in, but it was so dark in the stone structure that even with it, she was having trouble keeping track of her target.

The chamber lit up like the sun, making Mila turn her face away. Looking from the corner of her eye, Mila could barely pick out the tall robed figure, his arms hanging at his side and face upturned. A long screeching wail spilled from him along with a golden light that blasted out of the void where his face should be.

As Mila's eyes adjusted to the bright light, she got a better look at what was happening.

The device hadn't fallen into his face forever, like Mila half-thought it would. Instead, it seemed lodged in the center of the black void, hanging there despite not touching anything physical. The device's many lines glowed with celestial light, making it look like it was having trouble containing the power and threatening to burst at its many seams.

It was working. The power was overwhelming him. Now, it was only a matter of time.

Finn pulled his hand from the sand and inspected the structure he'd forced out of the ground. At a twenty-foot base, it took up a fair amount of the open space of their perimeter mines, but they still had room to move.

As he'd erected the pyramid, Azoth's army poured out of the portals. Within seconds, there were thousands of men and women charging toward them, but Finn had told them what to expect and was glad to see they were keeping their heads.

The masses kept pouring from the black rips in space-time, but anyone outside the perimeter was of little concern. It was the half-dozen portals inside the perimeter that were the real worry. Luckily, the closest ones seemed to be for the Rougarou and thralls, leaving the bewitched charging for the stasis mines.

"Danica, pick a portal and focus on it. Remmy, watch her back and take anything that gets past me." Finn looked at the dozens of minions coming out of the closest portals. "Victoria, you and I are the heavy hitters. Cause enough damage that they focus on us," he shouted before bellowing a dwarven war cry and sprinting for the closest cluster of enemies.

While sliding across the last five feet of sand, Finn slashed Fragar through the three thralls who were still getting their bearings. Several runes etched into the blade flashed with purple dwarven magic. One made the axe five times as heavy as normal for a split second, increasing its momentum. Another rune blasted high pressure air from the back of the single hooked blade, increasing the speed of the swing. And the final rune replaced the razor-sharp edge of the blade with the exact same blade from the moment before it sliced into the first thrall.

The effect was undeniable, and a prime example of why dwarven-made weapons were sought across the universe. Fragar had sliced three people clean in half in one swing while not slowing down and came out the other side as sharp as it had been before the strike happened.

There was a reason Finn had traded a literal moon for it. And not one of those barren pockmarked bastards—this was a full-on livable planet-type moon. Think Endor, minus the teddy bears.

Fragar was worth every stone.

A *whomp!* thudded through Finn's chest, followed by three more in quick succession. He lopped the head off one Rougarou while blocking the slashing talons of another with his prosthetic arm and glimpsed of the stasis mines activating.

A band of about twenty bewitched humans ran into the perimeter, their eyes red and swollen, and facial expressions blank if not a little sad looking. One of them crossed through the space above the converted hockey puck, and a sphere of constantly swirling white and blue almost instantly went from nonexistent to a globe forty feet across.

The bewitched people were stuck in that moment of reality, not blinking or twitching or even breathing. Time had stopped for them and wouldn't resume until the mine ran out of stored power.

Finn took the opportunity to test a theory, and instead

of blocking the second attack from the Rougarou, he side-stepped it. The swing hit no resistance and made the eight-foot-tall wolfman stumble forward. Finn grabbed it by the shoulder and sent a jolt of magical energy through his prosthetic while digging his finger into the tough hide until he gripped bone.

The Rougarou slashed at him with its free claw, but Finn batted it away, then spun in a circle while dragging the large beast around with him and picking up momentum. On his second rotation, Finn released his grip and threw the creature a good twenty feet, directly into one of the stasis fields.

Finn was a little surprised how deep it went before becoming stuck. He guessed it was ten or twelve feet. That was good. It gave him a way to deal with any bewitched that got through.

He checked on Danica and Remmy and saw that they were holding up well, and a truly deadly combination. Danica was making good use of the quiver that Mila had bought and Finn and Penny had modified for her. It used the same rune that replaced Fragar's blade, but this one was manually activated and basically refilled itself with a copy of itself from when it was full.

Danica hit the button on the quiver as she loosed her last arrow and the quiver was instantly full again, but all the arrows she had shot vanished as well. The same thing happened with the axe—he simply never saw the blade disappear as the new one showed up.

Finn was surprised by how effective focusing on one portal was. Danica by far had the most kills of them all. She shot every thrall and Rougarou dead within a step of the portal. There were so many dead that the portal itself was becoming blocked, and anyone coming out ran into a chest-high mound of their dead comrades. Eventually, the portal closed and wasn't replaced with another.

Danica picked another portal and started the process over.

Remmy was like a devil. She would appear for a few seconds to catch her breath, but Finn saw that she was taking his instruction to heart and had slowed her mad rush into a fluid dance, conserving oxygen and stamina. She could stay invisible for nearly a minute between reappearing. While she was unseen, she could slash down ten or twelve enemies with quick, precise hits. Even the towering Rougarou weren't safe from the small goblin. They took more hits, but that was only a matter of time for Remmy.

Finn fell into a rhythm. He kept his berserker rage at bay for now since this battle was about controlling the masses, not killing as many as he could in the shortest time.

He slashed the arm and head from a Rougarou, then chopped down a thrall with an overhand blow. Punching a wolfman in the ribs while sending a jolt of magic into the arm made it hit twice as hard. The Rougarou coughed up blood as his torso caved in, then fell, his heart crushed by his chest.

Victoria was like an angel of death, sliding into and out of groups of enemies like a dancer. Everywhere she went, creatures and thralls fell by the handful. Her dance of death played out with a placid face of pure experience. Thousands of years of battle had beaten her into a fine-tuned killing machine.

The battle was going well, right up to the point where the stone pyramid exploded.

Mila's smile quickly faded when the bright celestial light became shrouded with a black miasma that poured from Azoth's void of a face.

His scream slowly died as the light became darker. Then that thick oily smoke rolled around itself and flowed back into the void. In seconds, the device was nothing more than a pinprick of light in a roiling mask of infernal magic.

Mila was ten feet away from Azoth in the relatively small interior of the pyramid, and she felt his power growing by leaps and bounds. She immediately realized her mistake and fired several bolts from the Ivar to land at least a few hits before it was all over.

Azoth didn't raise a shield. Instead, he took the hits to the chest. The exploding bolts of magic blew his robe to charred shreds. He shrugged the garment off, revealing where bloody chunks of his stone-colored flesh had blown free, but they were healing before Mila's eyes.

She had only seen him without the robe one time before and that was from a distance. This time, he was on full display. His oddly smooth-skinned torso led down to a mass of hundreds of black and purple tentacles that seemed to be in constant motion, even when he stood still. But his most disturbing feature, his void face, now looked far worse with Mila's short-sighted failure on display.

The roiling black miasma flowed outward from the center as it enclosed the device. Then, less than an inch from the glowing core, it rolled back and flowed into the edges of his void. With the pinprick of light at the center of the smoke and the way it constantly moved in a donut-like pattern, it made looking directly at his face feel like falling down an endless pit.

"I should thank you," he rumbled. "I worried at first, but this turned out to be a pleasant surprise. A fitting gift for your new god."

"Go to hell," Mila growled while firing a constant barrage from her pistol, even forcing more magic into the already-stressed weapon. The bolts grew brighter and thicker, and when they hit they did more damage, but it wasn't enough. Azoth was letting her do it to prove how ineffective it was. He started laughing and spread his arms wide.

Mila growled and lowered the gun to her side. "Fine. I give up." She slipped the Reaper's case off her back. "Here. Take it and get the hell off my planet."

She held out the case and walked toward him. He seemed surprised and let her get as close as she liked.

"A wise choice, ch—"

Mila tossed the case at his feet—or tentacles, in this case—where it popped open, revealing nothing more than an empty case.

When he followed the falling case with his sorry excuse of a face, Mila reached up with lightning-quick reflexes and grabbed the device as the thick oily infernal magic ate her flesh.

She screamed as pain unlike anything she'd ever felt ripped through her body.

Azoth backhanded her across the chest, sending her flying into the slanted far wall. She hit hard and slid down it in a crumpled heap, becoming wedged between the wall and the ground.

"How dare you?" he screamed, sounding like metal sheets being torn in half.

Mila only had a second to shield herself as Azoth sent a large black-and-purple orb striking across the space and exploding against the wall, the ground, and her shield.

The sudden sunlight blinded Mila as she tumbled through the air along with melon-sized chunks of stone.

Solid and familiar arms caught her before she slammed into the ground and set her on her feet.

"You okay?" Finn's eyes locked on the Drude, who surveyed the situation with a calm posture.

"Not even a little, but I'm unhurt." She looked at him with a worried expression. "I fucked up. The device is feeding him. He's already too powerful for me to hurt, and he's getting stronger by the second. How's it going out here?"

As she asked, one of the stasis fields flickered then failed, setting loose the hundreds trapped in it. Finn dropped to his knee and quickly fed power into the ground, and the field snapped back up, recapturing all but a handful who had slipped past.

They exchanged worried looks. This was going down the toilet fast.

"I need to get that device from him. We can't let it feed him any more than it has. When I tried, his magic burned straight through me. I couldn't get it out."

Finn frowned. "I can try, but someone has to keep the perimeter going or we'll be overrun in seconds."

A teleport bubble popped right in front of them and Rebecca was there with a wand out and looking around with wide eyes.

"What the fuck, Rebecca?" Mila shouted as she jumped forward and chopped down a thrall that was diving for the woman. Victoria slid by, killing six more thralls on Rebecca's other side before disappearing into the melee once again.

"Mila! Penny told me the device will only feed Azoth's power. You can't use it on him!"

Mila saw Azoth aim at Rebecca's turned back. Stepping forward and putting herself between the two, she raised a shield as another orb streaked across the rubble-strewn field. This time, instead of trying to stop the blast Mila deflected it, sending the orb arcing off into the distance where it blew the top off one of those little mountains.

Mila looked over her shoulder with gritted teeth. "A little late for the warning, but we're working on it."

Yaminah stepped out of the portal behind Azoth and made eye contact with Mila. The scarred woman gave her a questioning tilt of her head. Mila nodded ever so slightly.

"I need you to take care of the stasis fields. They're quickly running out of power and Finn has his hands full," Mila directed, only then noticing that he'd stepped away to take out a large group of thralls.

Rebecca pulled out a second wand and pointed it at a

Rougarou as she uttered a short chant. The creature suddenly folded up into itself as if it had imploded. "What are you going to do?"

Mila set her jaw and started running toward Azoth. "Whatever it takes."

CHAPTER TWENTY-EIGHT

Mila charged across the battlefield. Her speed let her sidestep the minions blocking her path. She would have cut them down, but she'd put her weapons back in their holsters since she needed her hands free for this.

Yaminah had begun her intricate spell before Mila had taken her first step, but it was taking a while. Mila worried that it wouldn't happen in time, or maybe Yaminah was drawing her in for her master. No, Yaminah hated Azoth as much as Mila did—probably more.

Mila decided to trust the woman's hatred for their common enemy instead of doubt her choice to trust.

At the last second, Yaminah's spell finally activated. Mila was already leaping through the air, her feet coming up to hit Azoth in the chest. As Mila had predicted, he simply stood there, thinking himself invincible. It couldn't have been a better opportunity.

Chains as thick as Mila's forearm and fifty feet long shot out of the ground in a circle centered on Azoth like the spikes of a crown. Before the Drude could comprehend what was happening, the chains whipped around like a tornado, their ends still anchored in the earth, and wrapped themselves around his entire body, leaving only his head and shoulders exposed.

Azoth bellowed with rage and Mila saw him straining against the bonds, but another line of power from Yaminah pulled the chains back into the earth, making Azoth bend backward and taking away most of his leverage.

The move made for a perfect landing platform.

Planting her feet on his shoulders, Mila landed in a crouch and slapped her left hand onto the top of his head for stability. Cocking her right arm back, she formed her fingers into a claw.

"Pride before the fall, motherfucker," she growled before plunging her hand into the void of his face and grabbing hold of the device.

This time, she'd prepared for the agony although it didn't make it hurt any less. She fought through it while pulling with everything she had. She used her legs to push against his shoulders as she screamed with effort and pain.

Like a stuck door, when the device came loose it did so all at once, launching Mila off Azoth and onto her back a dozen feet away. She landed awkwardly, half on a chunk of the destroyed pyramid, and knocked the wind out of herself.

She realized that the burning pain wasn't leaving her right arm, and when she looked down, saw that the device was still glowing and dumping raw magic with reckless abandon. It was celestial magic, and more than half was hers coming back to her, but it was still raw power, and her body was still a living thing.

The sound of a minor explosion made Mila look up as Azoth broke a second chain, the links shredding with a loud boom as they failed all along their length. The next chain was off a second later, and the next in half that time.

Before Mila could get to her feet, Azoth was free and turning his wrath toward Yaminah. The poor woman had done everything she'd promised she would, and now she would pay the ultimate price—and there was nothing Mila could do about it. They might have stopped him from gaining more power, but he was already more than they could handle.

He raised a stone-gray hand while building an orb that would end her life.

Yaminah didn't look up at her slaver. Instead, she looked at Mila, her eyes pleading for help. The look was mixed with betrayal. Not for Azoth, but for Mila.

Mila channeled everything she had into a single blast of pure celestial magic. She didn't bother trying to hold back. This was an all-or-nothing sort of moment.

She felt the swirling energy coalescing into a single attack that would raze a building to its foundations.

Before Azoth could send his orb into the cowering Yaminah, Mila let loose.

The sheer size of the blast made Mila's eyes widen, not believing she had caused it. A six-inch-thick beam of pure white light tinged with gold lanced out from her palm and slammed into Azoth's lower back, lifting him off his feet and sending him tumbling across the sands. He slid to a stop only a few feet from one of the stasis fields.

Mila climbed to her feet, her back feeling like she'd beaten it with a club.

A scream of mad rage turned Mila's attention to her left, where she saw Missy climbing to her feet. Her chest was bloody, and the t-shirt she wore had a hole right through the middle where the bolt from the Ivar had blasted her out of the fight. Not enough out of the fight, it seemed.

The madwoman lifted her silver sword like it was a baseball bat and not a precision weapon. She continued to scream as her wings erupted from her back, the black having taken the entire wing instead of the half it used to be.

The sight made Mila cringe with sadness, then made her realize how defenseless she was without her power. She had used everything on Azoth. Mila knew she couldn't produce a shield strong enough to stop a BB gun, let alone a swing from the mad Valkyrie.

Luckily, she wasn't the only Valkyrie on the field.

Victoria shot past Mila like a comet, her golden wings springing to life and spreading wide. She slammed into Missy so hard that it made the sand at Missy's feet jump into the air.

The two Valkyries slammed into the ground and blasted a foot-deep crater into the sand.

Mila suddenly realized how vulnerable she was. She had nothing. Spotting Finn fighting off four enemies at once, she noticed that he dipped to the ground and swiped a bare hand through the sand. Purple energy leaped to his fingers before going back into the ground. A spike of stone shot out of the sand a second later and impaled two of the four, letting him handle the last two with ease.

When she looked down at the device in her hand, she was shocked to realize that it didn't hurt to hold anymore, then became worried that she'd done some kind of permanent nerve damage. She pushed the concern away and focused on the device in the same way she had when filling it.

She knew it shouldn't work like this for a Valkyrie, but over the last couple of days, she'd had to admit that she was more than that now. She didn't know why or how, but she knew it was the truth. If Finn could pull in magic, then she could, too. At least, she hoped it was like that.

Focusing on the device, she tried to do the exact opposite of what she'd done to fill it. It was awkward and her brain didn't want to let it happen, but Mila needed it to. She demanded it.

And then it did.

Power flooded into Mila. She felt her abilities return and her body heal, then she shook with potential. In a second, she had all she'd lost, and it was still coming.

She quickly realized that she needed to use it or it would burn her out. Like a light bulb with too much power, she would burn bright then pop.

Searing pain exploded in Mila's side as the impact threw her to the ground, her arm snapping as she slammed into another piece of rubble.

Rolling onto her back, she saw Azoth slithering toward her, his hands already glowing with more power.

Mila tapped into the overwhelming flow of magic

coming from the device and healed her broken arm almost instantly while simultaneously putting up a shield.

Two balls of infernal magic slammed into the barrier. It flickered, but was far from failing.

Mila scrambled to her feet and sent another blast at Azoth, but he raised a shield and absorbed the incredible amount of power like it was nothing. They traded blows back and forth, but neither of them could do much damage.

Azoth aimed another orb at her and she strengthened her shield, but at the last second, he turned and sent the bubbling black projectile at Yaminah.

The woman was still recovering from her last spell and was slow to react, but she turned a fatal blow into only a serious wound by rolling to the side. The orb aimed at her chest hit her right arm and side instead. The explosion sent her tumbling away, blood freely flowing from the wounds.

"No!" Mila shouted, redoubling her efforts and sending blast after blast at Azoth, but he blocked them all.

A stasis field flickered and failed behind the Drude, dropping several hundred bewitched people to the ground. Mila couldn't believe her eyes when she saw Carl and his team at the head of the group.

Mila dropped to one knee and pressed her fingers into the ground like she'd seen Finn do earlier. She didn't know what she was doing, but she kind of forced her power into the mine. It snapped back on, catching most of the bewitched, but she didn't see the G.A.E.L. team anywhere in the stasis bubble.

Azoth took the distraction as an opportunity to strike and hit Mila on the shoulder with an exploding orb.

Sending healing magic to the wound before she hit the ground, Mila watched as another stasis bubble failed, then another. She sent magic through the ground and the fields popped back up. Looking for Rebecca, she saw her struggling to fight off a Rougarou and charge a flickering stasis bubble.

The entire battle was turning into a clusterfuck.

She needed to do more. This trading blows wasn't going to cut it. There was no way they could win a battle of attrition.

Mila caught movement in the sky, but was forced to block another attack from Azoth. Mila raised a shield, but saw him turn toward Yaminah a split second later. She bunched up her legs, sprang forward and slammed her shield into the Drude, sending him skittering across the sand. Mila took the chance to charge in while his guard was down, but she saw Rebecca being overrun and diverted the attack meant for Azoth to a group of five thralls, giving Rebecca some breathing room.

By the time she turned back, Azoth was charging her.

"Come the fuck on!" Mila shouted, frustration almost overwhelming her. "Can we get a break? Just once?"

It was right about then when the four remaining Valkyries landed in flashes of light and brandished weapons.

"Need a hand?" a muscular woman of Indian descent asked before chopping a Rougarou's head off with a giant two-handed sword.

"Like you wouldn't believe," Mila answered, relief flooding into her.

"Take that asshat down, Mila!" Victoria shouted, her

sword locked with Missy's as they struggled for dominance. "We can take care of the rest. And for God's sake, don't hold back!"

Mila focused on Azoth, who seemed amused that they'd received some backup.

"All right, bitch. Let's dance." Mila gripped the device tightly and prepared to do something insane.

CHAPTER TWENTY-NINE

Mila didn't hold back.

She gripped the device and pulled the power out, filling herself far beyond her normal capacity.

Her wings exploded out of her back, far bigger than they used to be, and bright enough that they hurt to look at. She continued pulling in power while she focused on Azoth, who had slowed his charge and now had a cautious posture.

"Do I finally see a challenge from you, child?" he sneered, throwing an orb at her.

Mila formed a small shield over her hand and batted it away like it was a toy. She did the same with the next three. The entire time, she was pulling in power at an ever-increasing rate.

Power bubbled and spilled out of her as she reached her absolute limit. Light poured out of her eyes, rising and swirling like smoke.

She aimed with one hand and pulled Gram out with the other. The sword unfolded, then burst into white flames.

Azoth saw the writing on the wall, but he still had some tricks of his own.

He lunged forward, wrapped his hands around her forearms, and began to devour her. He pulled out everything she was, or at least tried to, but she used the opportunity to learn instead of blasting him away from her.

She felt what he was doing, learned how it flowed from her into him and finally how he changed that power to something he could use. She let him take far more than a full charge since she wanted to be sure she could do the same to him when the time came.

Azoth was the one to break the contact and stumble back, drunk on the power he'd stolen. He clapped his hands together and sent four incorporeal tentacles lashing out of the ground to wrap around her ankles and wrists.

The tentacles were far stronger than Mila thought they would be, but she was overflowing with power. She pushed raw celestial magic into them, attempting to burn them out at their source, but Azoth hadn't finished.

He made a series of complicated hand movements and shouted a word she didn't understand. She screamed as a pillar of swirling black flames engulfed her from below.

Her clothes instantly incinerated. Even the enchanted leather didn't stand a chance in the unnatural heat. The scream ripping from her throat cracked as the pain pushed her beyond her limits. The oils in her skin were superheated and fried her from the inside out. Every hair on her body flashed into smoke.

The only reason she hadn't instantly turned to nothing but a little pile of carbon was that she'd already been healing her body. The stresses of holding so much power were literally tearing her body apart, so a portion of that power had been continually healing the damage.

She dumped more healing into every corner of her body, and to her surprise, she healed faster than the fire could damage her. In seconds, she was fully healed despite the flames continuing to lick at her. Mila decided she'd had enough of this ride and sent a surge of power down the tentacles holding her aloft.

A ripping metal scream came from Azoth, and the fire cut off as he stumbled back while clutching the sides of his head. His many tentacles became uncoordinated in his distress, and he fell back onto the sand.

Mila stalked forward while gripping the device harder and sucking every last drop of power from it. The flow was increasing—she'd already replaced the power it had taken to heal the fire damage. Her body glowed as she ran out of places to store the power so it spilled out onto her skin.

She stepped close to his squirming tentacles and finally sucked the last of the power out of the brass ball. As soon as she did, the device came apart and fell to the sand in twenty separate pieces.

Staring at the creature that had caused so much pain and death in such a brief time and seeing fear radiate off it made her feel nothing but disgust.

"You should be braver," Mila told him. "You live a life where you torture and enslave and use and murder, and now, when you face a small taste of what you do to others, you cower. At least have the backbone to accept that over your life, you've earned this true death."

Mila pointed her finger at his void. "Is that it? Nothing to say?"

"Defend me," he shouted.

The sound of a rifle firing made Mila flinch, but she had already healed the gunshot wound. She turned to see Carl and his team, their guns pointed at her. She threw up a shield as they all opened fire.

Anger burned through Mila. She sent out a blast of celestial magic that washed over the team and several other bewitched people in their proximity. Every one of them blinked, then looked around in confusion as the spell shattered.

"Mila?" Carl asked. "What happened to you?"

"Hello, Carl. Sorry, I have to take out the garbage. If you could find Finn and see what he needs, that would be great."

He hesitated while looking from her to Azoth and back. "About time. That piece of shit is like the turd that won't flush."

Mila snorted. "I like that. It's super accurate, too."

"You know you're naked, right? Also bald... Everywhere." Nick gave her a confused once-over.

Tina slapped him. "What the fuck is wrong with you? She's obviously riding the edges of godhood, man. You want her to erase you for being a dumb fuck?"

"Sorry, ma'am." He cracked a salute.

Mila chuckled and shook her head. "It's fine—"

"How dare you belittle me in fr—" Azoth started, but Mila stomped on his lower abdomen with quite a bit of magical enhancement behind it.

"Shut the fuck up. The grownups are talking," she growled down into his face hole.

"Fuck." Nick backed away. "I think we'll leave you to it, then."

"We'll talk later," Mila told Carl.

He nodded and ran off to find Finn, gunning down a Rougarou on the way.

Mila turned back to Azoth. "You're a pathetic stain on the boot of the universe. You're cruel, and sadistic, and deserve a million times more than what I'll do to you. But I want you to know something before you know nothing, ever again. I don't want to make you suffer. I don't want to hurt you. I don't want to get my revenge. All I want is for you to not exist. You're a sickness, and the only thing you do to a sickness is eradicate it."

"I'll be back. It might take ten thousand years but we will face one another again, and I'll have fun peeling the skin from your—"

Mila reached down and grabbed him by the arms, lifted him to a standing position, and shook him. "Shut the fuck up."

Then she began.

She reached into the Drude and copied what she'd learned as he tried to devour her. She took his power away, changed it into something useful and kept it for herself. Her power grew even further.

It was easy.

There was no limit to the flow between them. She could take as much as she liked and she could take it as fast as she wanted, so she did.

Azoth didn't make a sound. He twitched and tried to hide away bits of his power, but she had come into his house and was opening all the drawers. She rooted out everything he had. When he ran dry, he started pulling it out of his minions.

The Rougarou fell first. All at once, the beasts went from flesh and blood to black dust that was instantly lost in the fine black sands.

Next were the thralls. They fell to dust as well.

Mila grabbed that reclaimed magic as soon as it flowed into him.

The mass control spell came next, leaving several hundred thousand people confused and scared, but still alive.

Missy and Yaminah were the last ones freed of their servitude. Both women immediately passed out, finally able to sleep without nightmares.

Then it was all gone. She took one last look, but Azoth was nothing but a body, devoid of magic.

Conversely, Mila was about to kill herself with too much magic. She needed to do something with it, and she needed to do it quickly. Looking down at Azoth's pathetic form slumped in her hands, she realized killing him wasn't enough. She needed to erase him.

Mila created a shield around Azoth and let the weak body slide to the bottom of the sphere before sealing it. Then she filled the shield with fire so hot that it burned the ash to nothing. For a brief second, there was a mini sun in the center of Iceland.

When she released the shield, not even dust fell out. He was gone. Truly gone.

She was dying. Mila knew it, but she didn't really know what to do about it. She had more power in her at that moment than ten thousand magicals combined, if she had to guess. She couldn't simply let it go—it would kill everyone on the island.

She cocked her head. "The Drude can do it... Whatever it takes, right?"

Mila closed her eyes and looked for a place she hadn't been since the first day she'd found out she was a Valkyrie. To her surprise, she found it easily.

Where do you keep ten thousand magicals' worth of magic? Elsewhere, of course.

CHAPTER THIRTY

Mila woke up feeling refreshed. Which was good, since she didn't remember how she'd gotten into bed. The last thing she remembered was stuffing a bunch of raw magic into another dimension to save for later.

"You're awake." Victoria closed the novel she was reading. She was reclining on the bed beside Mila. "So you don't freak out, you're still hairless. We need to get a hair potion, but they can be hard to find."

Mila reached up and felt her unusually smooth scalp. "Thanks. I definitely would have freaked out."

Victoria sighed. "Okay, I have to ask. What the hell did you do?"

"What do you mean?"

"I mean, you were getting your ass kicked, then turned into an unstoppable demigod. How?"

"Oh. I took all the power we put into the device back into myself so I could use it all at once."

Victoria raised an eyebrow. "That's not possible."

Mila chuckled. "I know."

Victoria sighed and climbed off the bed. "I'll go get Finn. He's still at the site, trying to sort out what to do with nearly three hundred thousand forcefully awakened Peabrains."

"They all remember?" Mila sat up in the bed.

"Yeah, it will be a real mess. Go take a shower or something. It'll be a little while."

Mila decided that was a good idea. Despite not having any hair at the moment, she felt oily, which kind of creeped her out.

She took her time in the shower, letting the hot steam and water wash the last few weeks away. She didn't want to have to go through anything like that ever again. That thought made her laugh. She would have to go through something like that again, for sure. It was her life now.

When she stepped out of the shower, she discovered that someone had gone back to the condo and grabbed more of her clothes, and left them in a bag on the counter. Digging through, she found a pair of black leggings and a gray V-neck t-shirt, and literally kissed them both before putting them on.

"Oh, how I've missed you two," she said to her clothes.

She also saw that someone left her a stylish black knit cap that made her look kinda cute, considering she didn't have any eyebrows.

When she walked out into the guest room, Finn was already there and sitting on the bed, a big, goofy smile on his face. "Hey, baldy."

"Hey, jerk," she retorted seductively.

"So, we have a surprise for you." Finn couldn't contain his smile.

"This sounds scary."

"Oh, it's terrifying. But you'll love it."

He went to the door and let Danica in. She had a white baby blanket over her shoulder and folded into her arm. Penny rode on her other shoulder, her smile nearly tearing her face in half.

"Oh, my God. Are you shitting me?" Mila practically skipped over and peeked into the blanket.

Inside were three baby faerie dragons, each with their eyes still closed, and laying piled on top of one another. Mila noticed the one on top of the pile was quite a bit smaller than the other two, but otherwise looked fine.

"This big girl is Tarra, and this is her brother Rhys, and this darling little girl is Mia. Pretty sure she's named after you."

"Oh my God, Penny, they're beautiful." Mila gently rubbed Mia's tiny head.

"Also, I found out you were having all those pregnancy swings because of Penny. She can explain later, but I have to say it's insane." She looked up at Penny. "Insane. How does your race even exist?"

"Chi shee." Penny poked Danica in the nose.

"What did she say?" Danica asked suspiciously.

"She said, 'Because of people like you,'" Mila translated and kissed Danica on the arm, then reached in and held Mia's tiny hand. "So, I'm not pregnant? It was all some crazy side effect from these little ones?"

"How would I know if you're pregnant or not?"

"Because you're my doctor, dummy."

"How am I supposed to check if you don't come to the hospital?"

"Because you're my *magical* doctor."

Danica laughed. "You got me there."

"Well? Am I?" Mila threw her hands up.

Danica started laughing in earnest. "No, babe. You're not pregnant."

Mila chuckled along with her. "You're such a jerk."

"I think we need a bigger place." Finn nodded toward the babies. "What would you think about buying an island?"

"How are we going to buy an island?" Mila laughed.

"Well, I know of a few tons of gold and gems that no one's using."

THE END

Get sneak peeks, exclusive giveaways, behind the scenes content, and more. PLUS you'll be notified of special **one day only fan pricing** on new releases.

Sign up today to get free stories.

Visit: https://marthacarr.com/read-free-stories/

AUTHOR NOTES - CHARLEY CASE

MAY 24, 2020

Thank you for reading the final installment of the Lone Valkyrie series. In the beginning I wasn't planning on doing a series for Mila, but after book one of The Adventures of Finnegan Dragonbender, I knew that we needed to show Mila's growth as a Valkyrie if the next series was going to be as awesome as I wanted it to be. She became a real powerhouse over the last three books, and to be honest she needed to be to fill the shoes I have waiting for her.

I always find it funny how characters I write demand things from me, then throw a fit if I don't oblige. Reminds me of my cats...

So, we've been stuck in our houses for a while now, and like I said in my last notes, I'm kind of made for this. However, most of my friends are not.

I have a friend that lives on the other side of the country that I have known for longer than I have not. (aka more than half my life) He and I, along with our wives, go on vacation twice a year. Usually we go skiing in the winter and head off to Chincoteague Island in the summer. This year was no different.

At least it was planned to be no different.

In the winter they had a family emergency that kept them home so we missed out on seeing them. And it's not looking good for this summer due to the pandemic.

Now, you have to understand that I'm okay with this. Family emergencies happen, and apparently so do pandemics, but I'm an introvert. My friend is not... he is very much an extrovert and having to stay home is driving him insane. Literally insane.

To get his socializing in we started playing D&D over video chat. When we saw how successful that was, he wanted to add another day of D&D every week. Okay, that's fine. Then he wanted to do a happy hour on Fridays. I mean that's three days a week, maybe... What about playing some pub quiz games? We could do it on Saturdays! Uh... so four days a week?

You can see where this is going.

The other night me and my wife were laying in bed after a long night of hanging out on a video chat and she turned to me with a furrowed brow.

"I can't believe I'm about to say this, but I think I'm getting too much social interaction during the quarantine."

I sighed. "Yeah. Me too."

"I don't think I can do this anymore... if I have to get on one more video chat I'm going to jump out the window and start punching a tree."

Somehow, during a stay at home order we were sick and tired of seeing people. We both just laughed at the irony.

The whole thing made me realize that there are all kinds of people out there. My closest friend is not handling this whole thing very well. He's slowly going mad, as if he's snowed into a hotel and trying to write a novel. His wife is doing just fine, and I think that's making him even more insane. Me and my wife are all good, and that boggles his mind.

Yesterday I realized that while it's him that's going insane, it's our fault. The three of us are way to calm for him. He wants people to freak out with him just a little bit, and talking to us makes him think he's the odd one, when in reality the three of us are the abnormal ones.

My point is that I wasn't really thinking about how I was affecting my friend. I wasn't doing anything wrong, but it was still upsetting someone I care about. I mean how hard is it to talk to my friend?

I guess what I'm getting at is that I have to go; happy hour starts in twenty minutes.

I hope you all are having the best time you can during this hard time, and if you have an hour or three, maybe call up a friend and get drunk online with them.

All the best,
Charley

(5/24/2020
Boise, Id)

AUTHOR NOTES - MARTHA CARR

MAY 24, 2020

Have you heard of the Barkley Marathon? It's this crazy 120 mile+ race through the mountains of Tennessee. There's no markers on the race course, there's no chip timers (they use books and runners tear out the page along the course that corresponds with their race number – yeah, you heard me right), and for most of it there's no real path. Part of it even goes underneath a maximum security prison through an oversized pipe. It costs $1.60 to enter and a license plate from where you live and only 100 get chosen each year to try. Very, very, very few ever finish. If or when a runner quits, someone plays taps on an old bugle.

It was calculated by someone (because there's always someone who has to calculate everything) that the extreme up and down of the race is the equivalent of going up and down Mt. Everest… twice – and all in a weekend.

There's a cool documentary on Prime if you want to check it out for yourself.

Why bring it up? Well, there's a point all of the runners keep making – that just challenging yourself and trying changes you forever... for the better. It doesn't matter if you finish as much as you try with everything you have, and you walk away ready for the next challenge. A runner learns to slow down their brain and relish where they are, notice everything, and wonder... where exactly is my wall? Is it here? Or is it a few feet further?

As runners drop out, they become an elite support team for the runners who are left, encouraging them and giving sage advice. They all know the inner race that's still being run for someone and they want to help them go the distance, whatever that distance turns out to be.

It's a very personal journey.

I am an off again, on again runner. Right now I'm a walker working my way back to running but I can still remember tackling tough spots on a course after weeks of trying and walking away high on endorphins wondering, what else could I conquer if I just kept at it? Afterward, it made every other task a little easier, not just because I was willing to try a little longer, but I was willing to let go of thinking I knew the ending to the story or how the journey should look. I became willing to be present and give it all I had and see where it took me – instead of insisting on being the leader. That last part has been key for me.

The number of hours I have wasted pondering 'what if' questions – magical questions with no answer that can only eat up time. And everything I do in a day becomes elevated because I actually notice where I am and who I'm with and what's going on.

Okay, back to writing for me. My personal Barkley is to run an entire 5k and I'm hoping that I'll be able to do that right around when they can bring back races. But, the even cooler thing is that I'm enjoying the journey and not waiting for any destination. More adventures to follow.

If smart phones and GPS rule the world - why am I hunting a magic compass to save the planet?

Austin Detective Maggie Parker has seen some weird things in her day, but finding a surly gnome rooting through her garage beats all.

Her world is about to be turned upside down in a frantic search for 4 Elementals.

Each one has an artifact that can keep the Earth humming along, but they need her to unite them first.

Unless the forces against her get there first.

<u>**AVAILABLE ON AMAZON AND IN KINDLE**</u>
<u>**UNLIMITED!**</u>

OTHER SERIES IN THE TERRANAVIS UNIVERSE

The Adventures of Maggie Parker Series
The Witches of Pressler Street
The Adventures of Finnegan Dragonbender

Other books by Martha Carr

Other books by Charley Case

JOIN THE TERRANAVIS UNIVERSE FACEBOOK GROUP

FOLLOW TERRANAVIS UNIVERSE ON FACEBOOK

CONNECT WITH THE AUTHORS

Martha Carr Social

Website:
http://www.marthacarr.com

Facebook:
https://www.facebook.com/groups/MarthaCarrFans/

https://www.facebook.com/terranavisuniverse/

Michael Anderle Social

Michael Anderle Social
Website:
http://www.lmbpn.com

Email List:
http://lmbpn.com/email/

Facebook
https://www.facebook.com/TheKurtherianGambitBooks/